Big Rig

A JAKE SULLIVAN NOVEL

Big Rig

A JAKE SULLIVAN NOVEL

CHIP BELL

"I wish I was a big rig
Rollin' on home to you
I wish I was a big rig
A big rig baby,
Rollin' on home to you"

- "Big Rig"
  by Jimmy Buffett

DEDICATION

To my daughter Jennifer, my new de facto publisher.

ACKNOWLEDGEMENT

To Eve for all her hard work and for putting up with me; Deb Giles, an over-the-road driver, for her knowledge and expertise; and MeMe Selleck, the great lady who owns and operates The Quartzsite Yacht Club.

PROLOGUE

CHAPTER 1

1997

Newsflash: Former Russian General and Presidential Candidate Alexander Lebid stated in an interview that 100 suitcase-sized nuclear weapons, "are not under the control of the armed forces of Russia." The Governor of the Russian Federation stated, "Such weapons have never been created."

CHAPTER 2

1998

It was impossible for the headlights on the convoy of trucks to pick out all the ruts and rocks on the vehicle-made road they were traveling in Kandahar Province, Afghanistan.

Victor Tevlov, formerly of the Ukrainian Ministry of Science, was in the second vehicle, following a lightly armored vehicle with armed guards. In the back of his truck were eight wooden crates, which had followed a long trek from the Ukraine to their present destination. Tevlov had been a scientist, a nuclear engineer, an educator, and a believer in man and God . . . but all that was in his past. He had seen firsthand the corruption and the idiocy in the Russian military during his tours of duty in Afghanistan and had come to believe that all the efforts of his past life came to nothing, so here he was – an arms dealer – ready to sell to the highest bidder the contents of his crates, that would result in the deaths of millions.

As the convoy snaked its way through gullies and rock outcroppings, Tevlov was faced with an open expanse, a dim outline of the horizon stretching off in the distance, with unnatural shapes spaced at intervals before him.

After a flash of light temporarily blinded him, a clearing space was illuminated by the headlights of four vehicles, one a truck with a cloth-covered back, and the others three ancient military vehicles painted in desert camouflage.

When the lights came on, Tevlov's convoy came to a halt, and men from both sides walked into the clearing to face each other. All held some form of automatic weapons, save two, Tevlov and Tarif bin Al-Hasam, the local al-Qaeda "General".

Tevlov motioned for Al-Hasam to approach, and Al-Hasam raised his hand to tell his men to stay in place, as did Tevlov, as they made their way to the back of the truck in Tevlov's convoy.

Pulling down the tailgate and opening the flaps, Tevlov pulled off the lid of the crate nearest the door, which had been loosened for just this purpose, and showed Al-Hasam the contents. Al-Hasam consulted paperwork he pulled from the inside of his jacket and read the information stenciled on the exterior of the contents. He looked at Tevlov and nodded his head in the affirmative.

He backed up, looked at his men, and called out in Arabic. One of his men went to one of the transport vehicles and picked up a briefcase and brought it to Al-Hasam, who, in turn, handed it to Tevlov. Tevlov moved with Al-Hasam and his guard to the front of the convoy and opened the briefcase so the headlights could illuminate its contents. He studied the eighty million dollars in bearer bonds and nodded to Al-Hasam in the affirmative.

Not a word was spoken as the parties transferred the crates and returned to their vehicles, and Al-Hasam and his men drove off into the night. After they had departed, Victor Tevlov smiled to himself.

"Ten million per crate . . . not a bad price."

He had no remorse . . . those types of feelings had left him long ago, and he directed his men to turn their vehicles around and head back the way they had come. As he took his seat on the passenger side of the lead vehicle, he thought about swaying palm trees he had seen in the photographs of a small island in the Caribbean that he would soon own.

CHAPTER 3

2002

Stanislov Lunev, a high ranking GRU defector, verified existence of Russian "suitcase nukes" identified as RA115s, weighing 50 to 60 pounds, the batteries of which can last for years when connected to an electrical source, each capable of a 1 kiloton nuclear explosion.

CHAPTER 4

2003

Newsflash:　　Saudis captured several top level al-Qaeda operatives. One, Shaykh Nasir bin Hamin al-Fahd, confirmed that al-Qaeda negotiated with the Ukrainians for Russian nuclear devices.

CHAPTER 5

2004

Newsflash: A London based newspaper, *Al-Hayat*, reported that al-Qaeda had purchased nuclear weapons from a Ukrainian scientist named Victor in Kandahar, Afghanistan.

Present

10/9

CHAPTER 6

Ali Marsaka, as his New York driver's license identified him, was behind the wheel of a United Nations African Renewable Energy van, wearing a perfect copy of a United Nations employee badge, as he drove on Port Boulevard, entering Port Miami.

The sun was just beginning to set as he looked at his GPS, which took him to the warehouse district. He scoured the names and numbers until he found the one where he was supposed to pick up non-working wind turbine engines, which were to be refurbished and shipped back to Kenya. The warehouse was operated by South Florida Container Terminal and was guarded by one Richie Stancik, a retired New York City Police Officer.

When the van approached, Stancik slowly approached the vehicle and studied the driver, noticing a bead of sweat forming on his forehead.

"Evening," he said.

The driver did not reply, but handed over a manifest.

Stancik studied the manifest, taking his time, and then, after staring at the driver again, moved back to his guard shack, picked up a phone and made a call, and a forklift soon appeared with four suitcase-sized wooden crates, which were loaded into the United Nations van. The process was repeated and Ali Marsaka was given a form to sign, showing that he had received the lading that he had come for. Marsaka then executed a slow U-turn and began moving back to the road he had previously traveled. It was then that Stancik saw the license plate: 6TNGR8. Stancik recognized it as an older New York plate, not issued by the U.N., and there was something about it as he watched the van move away. His old police instincts came back to him, and thinking about the sweating driver, he repeated the numbers and lettering to himself, but did so phonetically, *"6TN Grate --- sixty and great. Could be a coincidence,"* thought Stancik. But it sure as hell looked like a personalized plate to him . . . and what was that doing on a United Nations van? Suspicious by nature and years of police work, he went into his guard shack to make a call.

CHAPTER 7

Ali Marsaka was high strung and the nervous type. Although there were many who did not want him involved in this project, he had performed well in the preparation for 9/11, but he was about to make a serious mistake.

Glancing down at the GPS to make sure he was moving in the proper direction, he took a turn around the corner of a warehouse building too quickly and crossed the center line only slightly, just enough to strike the left front fender of a red cab hauling a fifty-three foot trailer with the red words "Carpenter Transport" stenciled on its side.

The over-the-road vehicle was driven by Deb Giles, a company employee for many years. She had an excellent driving record, but Marsaka had moved into her line of vision too quickly and there was nowhere for her to go. She stopped the truck and exited the cab to check the damage. In the interim, Marsaka, who was panicking, reached underneath his seat for a weapon, and began backing up, all in the same motion. He could hear the woman yelling at him to stop.

"Hold on, pal! This is your fault! We need to exchange information! You're not going to put me on the hook for this!"

Marsaka considered shooting her dead on the spot, but came to the conclusion that would only cause more problems as he started to pull away.

Deb Giles immediately began snapping photographs of his van, her damaged left fender, and carefully took photographs of the driver as he pulled away. After moving only a few feet and realizing that she was taking his photograph, he slammed on the brakes and started to open the door . . . the handgun placed against his right thigh . . . when he heard the sound of sirens coming from the warehouse area where he had picked up his load. Looking at the foolish woman in disgust, he slammed the door shut and quickly pulled away, turning out of sight several feet down the road.

Deb Giles stood there with her hands on her hips, looking at the damage to her cab and cursing the United Nations driver as she waited for the sirens to approach so she could file a complaint with the proper authorities. Imagine her surprise when she found herself surrounded by vehicles, men jumping from them with guns raised and ordering her to her knees, all wearing bullet proof vests stenciled with "FBI", "DHS", and "Miami Dade County Police". As she knelt on the road in front of her truck, the only thought going through her mind was, "*What the hell have I gotten myself into?*"

CHAPTER 8

Ali Marsaka made his way back across Port Boulevard and drove to a storage facility. He took out the key card he had been given and swiped it at the gate, and the mesh fencing slowly slid to his left as he entered the facility and began his search for Bay 121. Arriving in front of it, he punched in a number on a keypad and the metal door rose, and he entered the bay. Turning off the van and exiting it, he shut the door, walked over to the wall by the entrance, and flipped the switch, which turned on a light that had been installed for his purposes. He knew that a drain had been dug underneath where the van was parked, as he checked the pressure washer that had been provided. A partition of two-by-fours of plywood had also been erected, on the other side of which was a small cot and a refrigerator, as it was in this location that he was to spend the night.

He took off his clothes and donned the plastic suit that had been left for him and started up the power washer, spraying the van again and again from the water source, a large tank affixed to one corner of the bay. Slowly the white of the van gave way to a shiny blue, and slowly but surely, white paint and United Nations lettering flowed under the van and down the drain. When finished, he called the number on the encrypted phone he had been given and explained that all had gone well and that he had picked up the cargo without incident and was ready to go. He laid down for a fitful night's sleep, worrying about the lie he had told and rehearsing in his mind what he was to do the next day.

CHAPTER 9

The person to whom he had spoken, known only as "Luis," also made a call, which was rerouted from cell tower to cell tower all over the world until finally reaching its destination in Havana, Cuba.

"Yes?" came the voice on the other end.

"I've spoken with the Arab shit. He has completed his task with no problem, and I have given him his instructions for tomorrow."

There was a laugh from the other end of the call.

"Not just a shit, my friend, but a lying shit. I'm afraid Mr. Marsaka had an accident after he picked up our cargo. Based upon information I have received from my inside sources, not only has he jeopardized being traced through the van, part of which he left on a semi-tractor trailer, but the bitch driving it took his photograph with her cell phone."

"I will go to his location and take care of this problem," said Luis. "I knew we should have used our own men in this."

"Be calm, be calm, my friend. We can use this to our advantage. Unfortunately, we must maintain our working relationship with our Arab friends, but we will change the script of this little drama when Marsaka arrives at your location tomorrow. I am working on something now and will forward it to you when it is completed. We will leave something for our American friends to find, and if we are lucky, it will lead them far, far away from our ultimate target."

Knowing full well what the Leader meant, a huge smile spread across Luis's face as he thought of the fun he would have tomorrow.

"I understand. I will great him warmly when he arrives tomorrow."

"Good," said the Leader, "I will provide you with instructions and the information and how to use it later tonight," and the line went dead.

"*Poor Marsaka, you little Arab shit. Not long for this world, I am afraid,*" mused Luis as he turned off the phone and went about his business in the huge warehouse he operated in Little Havana.

CHAPTER 10

Jake Sullivan and Mike Lang had only been back from their adventures in Montana for two weeks. Their task force had been in place for months, based upon chatter that nuclear weapons were going to be smuggled into the United States. Representatives of the FBI, DHS, the CIA, and the Department of Justice had gathered at Jake's office in the Federal Building in Miami as soon as the call had come in from Jess O'Donnell, the Director of Homeland Security.

"All right," said Jake, "you all know what's happening. This thing is for real. Let's see what we know," he said, pointing at Ted Forsythe, the SAC of the FBI office in Miami.

"We got lucky. Evidently a van disguised as working for the United Nations offloaded 8 wooden crates from a warehouse facility in Port Miami. A fast-thinking former New York City cop thought the license plate was peculiar and he ran it, and he was right. It was a vanity plate issued to one Benjamin Freedman, who got the plate when he bought a sports car and retired at age 60. Unfortunately, Mr. Freedman's been dead for six years, and the plate is out of circulation."

Mike lifted his head from an outline of the briefing he was reading.

"Sixty and great, huh? Smart thinking from our friend from New York."

Bob Porter from Homeland spoke up next.

"We immediately sent a team to check the warehouse. There was a high level of radiation residue present from where the crates had been sitting. It's the real deal."

John Severn from TSA spoke up next.

"My boys at one of the docks got lucky. Seems like the driver of the van was in a hurry. He took a corner too fast and collided with the front of a semi that was heading to the warehouses for pickup. The driver, one Deb Giles, started taking photos of the damage to the van and the truck because she thought he was trying to run away from the accident . . . and, got a great photo of him," and he threw an 8 x 10 glossy on the table. "Everything was downloaded from her phone and sent to Homeland."

"We know who he is yet?" asked Jake.

"Not yet," said Porter. "We're working on it."

"Do it fast," said Jake. "This could be the lead we need. Where's this Deb Giles now?"

"We had to process everything down at the dock. She was more concerned about her employer and the damage to the truck than anything else, but we're going to bring her here as soon as everything is done. She should be on her way now."

Jake looked over at Ted Ristik, representing the CIA in their little group.

"Anything new with the chatter out there?"

"Unfortunately, yeah. Something that I think pertains to this, and something I'm not quite sure of."

"What have you got?" asked Jake.

"We think we've pinged something in Pakistan. Best we can make out . . . the translation is, 'Phase one complete.'"

"Meaning they're here," said Mike.

"That's how we're taking it," said Ristik. "The thing we don't yet understand is an Arabic phrase. It keeps getting repeated over and over. Take a look," said Ristik, as he passed around a piece of paper that bore the notation "HADJIALIGHADAB 1015".

The members of the task force looked at the notation and looked at each other, and finally all eyes turned to Ristik.

"Any idea what it means?" asked Jake.

"One part . . . 'GHADAB' . . . means 'wrath', or 'fury' in Arabic. The first part we haven't figured out yet. Also, the 1015 could refer to October 15th, which is the feast of Eid-al-Fitr at the end of Ramadan."

"Shit!" said Mike, standing up.

"What is it?" asked Jake.

"I'm not sure. Let me check something out," and he picked up a binder and started looking through it. "1015 . . . 10/15 . . . October 15th."

The stares at Mike of everyone at the table turned to dread and finally, Ted Forsythe of the FBI gave voice to that dread.

"Christ! That's the date of the G8 Summit in Phoenix. That's their target."

Just then, Bob Porter's phone buzzed and he answered, "Good," and started writing on a pad. "All boots on the ground. Let's go," was all that he said and then hung up. "We know who he is," said Porter. "His name is Kareem Anwar . . . a low-end al-Qaeda soldier. Used to live in the Bronx. We suspected he had something to do with 9/11 but never pinned anything on him. He ran a little Muslim food store for years. We thought we had something and started to close in a couple years ago, but he went underground, and we lost complete track of him."

"Until now," said Jake. "And if he surfaced now, it's for something big."

"One other thing," said Porter, "the whole U.N. thing and the truck color might be a ruse. They did an analysis of the paint on the semi involved in the accident. Underneath the white paint was blue paint."

"So we could be looking for a blue van instead of a white one?" asked Mike.

"Exactly."

"Get all this information out right now," said Jake to everyone. "Get everybody you have on this. Tap all your resources. This is our lead, folks. We've got to find this guy . . . and find this van . . . whatever the hell color it is. We have five days. Let's move."

CHAPTER 11

Deb Giles had been right to wonder what she had gotten into. She had been taken in as something called "a material witness," they told her, and she was angry . . . very angry.

No one would listen to her. No one cared about her down time. No one cared about the damage to her truck. No one cared about what her employer was going to do if she didn't make the proper reports. All they cared about was the guy that hit her. They took her truck to God knows where, then took her to a room where she did interview after interview, explaining again and again that she didn't know the guy driving the van, the circumstances of what she was doing there and what she was going to pick up. Then, finally, they put her in the back of this black van and were taking her someplace that they wouldn't tell her. She put her head back as she sat there and closed her eyes and thought to herself, "*This was supposed to be an easy run. One pickup in Miami, a drop off in Raleigh, and back home to Virginia for a week off.*"

She thought she was allowed a phone call, but they informed her she wasn't in custody . . . but, of course, they also wouldn't let her go, so she had no way of telling her sister where she was or what was going on. She was tired, and she had to admit to herself that she was somewhat scared about what was going on . . . but more than anything, she was angry . . . and that anger grew as the vehicle stopped and she was led into the Federal Building in Miami and placed in, yet, another room.

CHAPTER 12

Deb Giles raised her head as she sat in the conference room with one large mirror, recording device, and a locked door. She knew that there were people on the other side of the mirror that could see her, even though she couldn't see them, and she raised her head when the door finally opened.

In strolled a man in a shirt and tie, sleeves rolled up, dark hair graying at the temples, a sort of smile that wasn't a smile, and penetrating blue, or maybe green, eyes.

"Miss Giles, my name is Jake Sullivan. I'm a federal prosecutor here in Miami."

"Prosecutor? Wait a minute!"

"Take it easy, Miss Giles. I'm not here to prosecute you. I'm here to thank you."

"Well that's something," said Giles.

"Look, I know that you have gone through a lot. I also know that you didn't do anything wrong and you have nothing to do with any of this, but unfortunately, the person that was in the accident with you is a person of interest in a potential terrorist threat to this country. We need to find him and we need to do it quickly. I've gone over your statements," he said, throwing a file in front of her, "and I've looked at the photographs you took, and we've identified this man. I just want to know if there is anything else you can tell me that you think might be helpful, given the situation."

Deb Giles looked at this Jake Sullivan. For some reason, she knew he was telling the truth, and her anger left her. She reread her statements and looked up at the ceiling and tried to concentrate.

"I don't know what else I can tell you. The accident happened so quickly. I wouldn't even have taken the pictures if he hadn't tried to run. Other than the damage to my truck, the damage to his van . . . he didn't even say a word. I mean, I gave him hell, but he never said anything."

"Can you tell me anything about the van he was driving that might give us some indication where he might be headed?"

"Just what I told the officers at the port. It was a United Nations van, so . . . all I can think of is he was going to go back to New York. I'm sorry, Mr. Sullivan. I wish I could tell you more, but I really can't."

Jake closed the folder from which he had taken her statements and sighed. He shook his head up and down.

"I understand," and he looked back in the folder. "Deb . . . can I call you Deb?"

"Sure," she said.

"I understand, Deb, and I appreciate everything you've done. What are your plans?"

"Well, I have to take my truck in to the Miami terminal, report the accident, fill out the paperwork, and they'll tell me what I'm supposed to do."

"Let me ask you this . . . given the situation, if I put in a word for you with your employer, do you think you could wait until tomorrow to do that . . . just in case we come across anything tonight . . . or even better, if we find this guy, maybe you can help identify him for us? And just in case we find out something about the accident we need you to explain? Maybe there's something that you didn't recognize as being important that is . . . I'd like to have you around for a little while so we can talk to you."

She looked down at the table and thought about it and looked back at Jake.

"You'll talk to my employer?"

"Absolutely, as soon as we leave this room."

"Sure, I can wait until tomorrow then."

"Thank you. We appreciate that. I'll tell you what, we have a place where we put people up where we can keep an eye on them and make sure that they're safe but keep them comfortable when things like this happen. I'm going to have a colleague of mine, Mike Lang, take you there to spend the night, and then we'll see if we can get this all taken care of in the morning."

"Well, it's not like I have a real choice, Mr. Sullivan, but like I said, I'll help in any way I can."

"Thanks again, Deb, and you can call me Jake. I'll talk to Mike and have him in here in just a couple of minutes and then he'll get you situated."

"Okay," she said, and under her breath again, "*not like I have a choice.*"

Day 1

10/10

CHAPTER 13

Ali Marsaka had left the storage facility early in the morning after the van had dried and he had been able to wipe it down, the midnight blue shining in the morning sun. He traveled the route his GPS directed him to take . . . a route that had few street cams and little traffic . . . and made his way into Little Havana, where he pulled up to a large warehouse door, which opened before his vehicle had even stopped. He pulled in and the door closed behind him.

The man he knew as "Luis" came up and shook his hand.

"Congratulations, my friend. A job well done. Let's see what we have," and he and Ali moved to the back of the van and Ali unlocked the doors and opened them, showing the eight crates sitting on two pallets, four on each, securely tied down to avoid as much movement as possible. "Well done," he said, "well done, indeed. Now we have to go make our next delivery," said Luis, slapping Ali on the back, forcefully enough to knock him forward. "Sorry, my friend, I'm just so excited about this great mission."

"Can I have some coffee before we go?" asked Ali.

Luis had noticed his hand shaking. He was beginning to wonder if Ali knew what was about to happen, but he let the thought pass. Even if he did, there was nothing he could do about it.

"Certainly, certainly . . . come this way. We'll both have a cup, and then we'll hit the road."

"Where are we going?" asked Ali.

"Up 95," he said. "We have to make them think we're heading north."

"I thought I <u>was</u> taking these packages north," Ali said, somewhat suspiciously.

"Yes, but we can't let them know exactly where," replied Luis, thinking quickly.

CHAPTER 14

Deb Giles had been put up in one of the federal safe houses in Miami – a little motel called the Sunset Inn, just outside of Coral Gables. She was awakened early in the morning with a sound near and dear to her heart. She looked out the window and there, along the roadway on the far side of the parking lot, sat her beautiful rig, and she knew she was going to be rolling on home.

Dressing quickly, she exited the motel room and headed across the lot, where Mike Lang was leaning against a black SUV.

"Thanks, Tom," said Mike to a man dressed in overalls who had driven the semi into the lot. "Go ahead and get in. I'll be right with you.

Tom nodded and entered the passenger door of the black SUV.

"Well, here she is, as promised," said Mike.

"So I see," said Deb. "I take it you don't need me anymore."

"Everybody wanted me to tell you what a help you've been. We haven't found this guy yet, but thanks to you, we know who he is and we'll get him."

"Glad I could be of some help," she said looking down at her feet. "I hope you do."

Mike smiled and held out his hand.

"Thank you again, Deb Giles, we appreciate it."

"You're more than welcome, Mike Lang," she said, smiling. "Tell Mr. Sullivan I thank him, too."

"I'll do that," and he turned away, but quickly turned back to face her. "Oh, one more thing . . . you can hop on 95 and head to your stop and then home to Virginia," said Mike. "This whole accident thing was taken care of with your employer last night. We suggested that instead of them giving you any hassle, they give you a commendation. You deserve it."

Deb smiled broadly.

"I don't know what to say."

"No need," said Mike. "Have a good trip."

He entered the driver's seat of the SUV and pulled out. She waved as he went by.

"Thanks again."

"Yessssss!" she said, pumping her fist. "Rollin' on home!" She went back into the room, showered, collected her things, and came out and climbed into the driver's seat of her rig, looked around, took in a big breath of that intoxicating smell she loved, slapped the steering wheel, put her rig into gear, and headed for the ramp for I-95 North.

CHAPTER 15

It happened at a simple intersection. On her left was the entrance to northbound I-95. She was in the left turn lane and was going to have to wait for the left turn light to come on. She had just missed the last one as she pulled up and traffic would start moving toward her on the steady green. She hit her turn signal and was waiting, looking across the street at the traffic facing her, and that's when their eyes met. A face she would never forget sat directly across from her in a midnight blue van that was beginning to move. It appeared he had a passenger with him, and instinctively she knew where he was headed, and she picked up her phone and tapped in the number she had been given the night before.

"Mike Lang," came the response on the other end.

"Mr. Lang . . . Deb Giles. He's here! He's trying to get on 95 North in a blue van!"

"Slow down, slow down! What are you talking about?"

"It's him! The guy you're looking for! I'm sitting right across from him at a traffic light . . . the entranceway to I-95 North right across from me . . . that's where he's headed! He's got somebody with him!"

"Slow down," again, Mike said. "Slow down, Deb, slow down. Give me descriptions as best you can . . ."

Luis, sitting in the van with Marsaka, had seen the exchange of looks between him and the girl driving the semi. It was her. He made a decision. They sped through the intersection and he yelled at Marsaka to stop. He slammed on the brakes directly across from Deb's open window. Luis pulled out a Glock 17, pushed Marsaka down, out of the way, and began firing, and Deb Giles' head exploded as it took two direct hits before she slumped lifeless over the wheel, and the truck slowly started to drift through the intersection and came to rest against a light post on the other side.

The phone had fallen from her hand but the sound of Mike Lang's voice still called out, "Deb! Deb! What happened?! Deb!," but Deb Giles never heard those words, and the last thought she had as she saw the weapon being raised and pointed at her was that she was never going to see Virginia again.

CHAPTER 16

By the time Jake and Mike arrived at the scene, the Police had already taped it off and techs from the various agencies were swarming the scene. The body had already been removed from the truck and zipped into a plastic bag.

Mike brushed past Assistant Medical Examiner, Mitzie Burke, to reach the body.

"Whoa! Slow down, cowboy!" she said, and when she got no response, looked questioningly at Jake. He touched her shoulder.

"Take it easy, Mitzie," he whispered, "this one's personal."

Dr. Burke nodded with understanding as she looked over at Mike, and she walked over to him and put her hand on his as he reached to unzip the bag.

"Mike," she said in a soft voice, "don't. You don't want to see this. She took two direct hits to the head. The best I can tell you is she died instantly. No pain."

Mike looked at her and slowly nodded and drew back his hand and walked away. Jake nodded at Dr. Burke, thanking her, and went after Mike.

"Mike, slow down."

Mike wheeled around at him.

"She didn't deserve this, Jake. She didn't know anything else. She couldn't cause him any harm. The sons-a-bitches didn't have to do this."

"I know . . . I know," said Jake, "and we'll get them, Mike. We'll get all of them."

"You're God damn right we will," said Mike, as he turned again and went to see what the techs had found.

CHAPTER 17

Luis had Marsaka drive the van up the I-95 North ramp, but only stayed on the route until the very next exit where they got off again, and Luis directed him from there. In the meantime, he got on the phone and made another encrypted call, explaining what had happened and the action he had taken.

"Unfortunate," said the voice on the end of the line, "but necessary, I realize. Move up our plans and head for the destination and do as I instructed. I'll make our compatriots understand why this action had to be taken . . . then we'll have them prepare the next leg of the journey."

"Understood," said Luis, as the line went dead, and he turned off his phone.

"What's going on?" asked Marsaka.

"Your part in this is almost over, my friend," said Luis. "We just confirmed arrangements that the next leg of the journey will be meeting us shortly, and then you can be on your way."

"So I'm not taking the items north?"

"No. Change in plans," said Luis as he directed Marsaka to pull into a wide space underneath an overpass and directed him to turn off the engine.

Marsaka's nervousness increased as he looked around him. There were no buildings, no people, no anything.

"This place is very isolated," he said.

"We're going to hand off the goods to someone else. Of course it's isolated," said Luis. "Don't worry, they'll be here soon."

"And what am I to do?" asked Marsaka.

"Well," said Luis, "things could have been different," as he moved the Glock in his hand slowly up as he talked, "but you see, they are what they are. You lied to us. This is all your fault. The accident, the photograph taken by that girl, the one who recognized you at the intersection, the one I had to shoot . . . all this is your fault."

"Please! Wait! I can explain," Marsaka said.

"You failed us, Ali. You put the whole mission in jeopardy."

"But I can explain!" he said. "It wasn't my fault."

"Ahh, that's where you're wrong," said Luis as he raised the Glock and shot Ali in the temple, brain matter and blood splattering out of the open driver's side window onto the pavement below. Luis smiled. "It was your fault. Evidently, you weren't listening to what I was saying."

Luis knew that the other truck would be there soon. He took out his knife and cut open the lining of Ali's jacket and stuffed the paperwork he had been sent inside. Taking a needle and thread he brought with him, he quickly sewed the lining back together and looked at his finished work. "*Not bad,*" he thought. "*They'll find it, but after all, that's what we want.*" He then exited the van and walked around the side, careful to avoid the blood and brain matter lying on the pavement. "*What a mess,*" he thought, shaking his head, and sat down on the base of a stone pillar, took out a cigar, lit it, and sat back and waited.

CHAPTER 18

"Mike and I are heading back now. Give me every cam you have on I-95 North. We're looking for a blue van, the shape identical to the U.N. van at the dock. The white paint was washed off. It's the same vehicle . . . same driver. We need to stop them before they get to their destination. Accompanied by a passenger, both armed and dangerous. Stop at any cost . . . understood? We're heading back."

Jake looked over at Mike, who had been quiet, looking out of the side window as they headed back to the Federal Building in Miami.

"You all right?" Jake asked.

"Another innocent life lost," said Mike. "You'd think I'd get used to it."

"Of course you won't get used to it," said Jake, "that's what makes us different from them."

Mike looked over.

"Sometimes I wonder about that, Jake."

"No you don't!" snapped Jake. "You're nothing like them, and neither am I. Do you think they care about what happens to people like Deb Giles? You said it yourself . . . he didn't have to kill her, but he did. It was a chance happening, Mike. She was at the wrong place at the wrong time . . . twice."

"Maybe we should have done more. Maybe we should have stayed with her."

"She wanted to go home, Mike. We set her free. We let her go. That's what she wanted."

"Yeah, I know," said Mike, "I know," and he shook his head. "What's next?"

"We go back and go everything again and again and we track these people down, and we take them out. That's what's next."

Mike looked over at Jake and nodded.

"I'm with you. Let's go."

CHAPTER 19

Luis had just finished his cigar when a tractor trailer pulled up. A brown cab with a silver trailer with one word on the side in dark brown script: "Southern".

A man got out of the cab, another foot soldier of al-Qaeda, and opened the rear of the trailer and pulled out two metal planks to form a ramp, and drove down a small forklift that was attached to the rear interior of the trailer. It only took a few minutes and two trips to reload and secure the 8 crates in the tractor trailer. He then used the forklift to randomly move other boxes inside to create a hap-hazard pattern, which would not allow the crates to stick out to a casual observer of the cargo. He then re-secured the forklift, slid in the metal planks, and closed and locked the rear of the trailer. He then looked at Luis.

"Follow the GPS," was all that Luis said, and the man nodded, climbed into the cab, and drove off, never having said a word the entire time.

He took I-95 North as far as Fort Lauderdale and stopped. After getting something to eat, he took a nap in the back of the cab. When he woke, he started driving, now on Interstate 10, heading West.

Day 2

10/11

Day 2

DMII

CHAPTER 20

Jake had stayed overnight on the cot he kept in the small room adjacent to his office, but sleep had not come. The call had come in after he and Mike had gotten back to the office and it had not been good news. The blue van had been found, Kareem Anwar was dead, but the cargo was gone. Their only lead had just become a dead end.

Jake was pouring a cup of coffee for himself when he heard the door open. Looking at his watch, he smiled and knew that Eva had just arrived. He turned as she approached.

"Jake Sullivan, did you get any sleep at all last night?"

"Some," he said.

"Don't lie to me. Listen . . . you need to be on your toes so you can solve this mess, and to do that, you need sleep."

"Sorry, Eva, some nights, sleep just won't come."

"Well, I suggest you go home and get some rest tonight. You're not going to be any good to anybody if you keep this up."

He looked at her and smiled.

"I promise."

"Sure you do," she said, raising her eyes. "Sure you do," and headed toward her desk. "No good news, I see," she said as she went through the logs from the night before.

"Damn little," he said, sitting down and rubbing his eyes.

The next one in was Mike, looking about the same as Jake.

"Oh, you too?" said Eva.

"Not now, Eva," said Mike, "not now."

She turned and shook her head, muttering to herself, "They never listen."

"We have anything?" asked Mike.

"Afraid not," said Jake.

"So, now what do we do?"

"I'm open to suggestions," said Jake.

"Pray?" asked Mike.

CHAPTER 21

It was never determined whether either of them actually prayed, but the call came in while the morning was still early.

"Jake, this is Ted Forsythe, FBI. We got something."

"I'm putting you on speaker," said Jake. "What is it?"

"Looks like a list. I'm on my way in. Better bring in everybody."

There was silence on the other end.

"I hope I'm wrong, but I think we just found a list of targets."

"Make it fast," said Jake. "I'll get everybody else here."

Mike looked at Jake.

"Did he say targets? Plural?"

All Jake could do was nod his head.

CHAPTER 22

Everyone knew they were on call, and it only took a half hour for the task force to assemble, and fifteen minutes later Ted Forsythe arrived.

"All right, here's what we have. This was concealed in the lining of Ali Marsaka's jacket."

He clicked a remote in his hand and a document appeared on the screen, clearly written in Arabic.

"Translation?" asked Jake.

"The top line is what you've seen before, 'HADJIALIGHADAB 1015'. GHADAB means 'wrath'. The words below it ..."

"You don't have to translate," said Mike. "I can read it."

"Yeah, unfortunately, I bet we all can," said Bob Porter of Homeland Security.

What shown on the board were Arabic names of eight cities in the United States: Jacksonville, Atlanta, Charlotte, Washington, D.C., Baltimore, Philadelphia, New York, and Boston.

"Eight crates," said Mike, "eight cities."

"My God," said Ted Ristik from the CIA, "they're going to blow up the whole east coast."

Jake was staring at the board.

"What the hell is the power of these things?"

Ristik answered, "There's a guy over at the Atomic Energy Commission . . . his name is Dr. Jason Rueben . . . doing calculations."

"See if you can get him on the phone," said Jake, "I want to talk to him."

While the call was placed, all eyes remained on the screen, thinking about eight great American cities lying in ruins. The disaster they didn't even dare think about as they combatted international terrorism, had now arrived.

"I'll put him on speaker, Jake," said Ristik.

"Hello," came a voice.

"Dr. Rueben?"

"Yes, sir."

"This is Jake Sullivan."

"Yes, Mr. Sullivan."

"I understand you've been doing some calculations based on information provided to you."

"I have."

"Can you tell us what we're looking at?"

"I can, Mr. Sullivan."

"Go ahead, you're on speaker. We're all listening."

"The best that we know, Mr. Sullivan, is that these suitcase bombs are in the 1 to 10 kiloton range. Just so you have something to relate this to, the uranium fission bomb dropped on Hiroshima was just over 10 kilotons. I tend to think that these bombs would be of a lower range, but I can't be sure. I'm going to tell you what a 1 kiloton bomb would do, and if you want to think the worst, you can measure it out ten-fold."

"Go on, Doctor."

"The mode of detonation is important, depending on what the intentions of the terrorists are. To be set off at high altitude would require some type of launch or aircraft, but that's normally intended for electromagnetic pulse, or EMP as we call it."

Mike spoke up.

"You mean it knocks out machinery, computers, anything electrical, over a certain area, right?"

"Exactly. It could knock out electronic command and control, but this isn't what terrorists usually do. They're not worried about a secondary attack. They're worried about creating havoc and fear, and to do that, the best thing to do is a ground burst. The blast itself causes great damage, but the big thing about the ground burst is that the buildings and geography maximize the production of fallout particles as they implode. When these particles are vacuumed up into the fireball, they're vaporized and become radioactive and then float down to the earth within hours. The only other thing is something in between . . . a low altitude strike, which would cause a combination of these effects, which creates a bigger fireball blast wave, like a ground blast and an air blast meeting. This would decimate cities and cause high numbers of immediate casualties, which is what they want, but they still have their mushroom cloud rising from the ground for propaganda purposes. I think the only way a terrorist could do this would be in some light aircraft flying over ground zero, which would be a suicide mission, or by some unmanned means."

"What are we looking at, Doctor?" asked Jake, "as to casualties and destruction?"

"I'm sorry, Mr. Sullivan, but it's horrifying. Initially there will be a split-second flash equal to a hundred suns, with intense heat that travels at the speed of light. As the fireball expands over a diameter of 460 feet, the center temperature will be 10,000°C. Metallic objects up to 450 feet from ground zero will vaporize, and up to 670 feet away will melt. People in these ranges simply cease to exist and become raw material for the later fallout. At 1,300 feet from ground zero, rubber and plastic will ignite and melt and wood will char and burn. Third degree burns a quarter mile away and second degree burns up to half a mile away and first degree burns up to nearly a mile away. Those that survive the melting effects of the heat radiation will be finished off by high winds at the city center – 670 miles per hour – which will level or damage even steel and concrete structures within 740 feet of the blast. No one will survive. When the wind speed drops to 380 miles per hour at about 1,000 feet, the tallest buildings will be lucky to be left standing and survivors of the heat pulse will suffer fatal lung injuries. As the speed drops to 225 miles per hour most dwelling houses will be destroyed and streets will be blocked by debris that become bombs themselves. Power lines, gas mains, and oil tanks will all be ignited. The fallout from one of these bombs will kill at least

50% of the humans exposed to it for an hour or longer. These areas will be uninhabitable for months, perhaps up to a year, and even after that there could be issues with radiation. Again, based upon the Hiroshima bombing and scaling down the bomb yield, you can expect fatalities of 20,000 in a major American city and a similar number of injured.

That's the best summation I can give you, based upon the information we have, Mr. Sullivan. The horror of such an attack is plainly evident . . . and remember . . . this is if the bomb is minimal."

There was a deep silence in the room as the numbers were calculated by each individual, as the devastation was imagined and the death and injury totals seared into the consciousness of those that sat there.

Jake cleared his throat and spoke.

"Thank you, Doctor."

"Don't thank me, Mr. Sullivan. I've given you the details of Armageddon. Don't thank me for that," and the line went dead.

Ted Forsythe was the first to speak.

"There's something else I need to show you, and as you're all probably aware by now, I've taken some unilateral action. These are scenes of the concrete area next to where the van was found. This first photo shows a fresh oil dripping on the pavement. Obviously, they had off-loaded the crates onto some other vehicle. We think we know what that is. There was a puddle that other vehicle would have had to drive through to get access to the van, and it left a tire print.

That tire print is for a tire used on tractor trailers. Assuming that oil spill was from the engine of the cab pulling that trailer, it looks like it's a 53 footer."

"Why would they need something that big for eight crates?" asked Mike.

"Well, we've come up with a theory, but it's only a theory. What if it's a real tractor trailer – not a phony – actually making deliveries up the north coast, but its driver is with al-Qaeda?"

"Shit!" said Jake, "they've mingled the crates in with actual goods being transported."

"Exactly."

"Any idea what company?" asked Mike.

"Not yet," said Forsythe. "Everybody's scouring traffic cams on the interstates, we have alerts out, and we have road blocks set. If we have to, we'll stop every single tractor trailer on the road. At least, that's what we think is now carrying these bombs."

"Nice work," said Jake, "nice work. All right everybody, let's get after it."

"The one thing we have to consider," spoke up Ted Forsythe, as everybody stood to leave.

"What's that?" asked Jake.

"First target on this list is Jacksonville. Given the time frame since that alleged tractor trailer picked this stuff up, he's been there already. We've got to mobilize everything we've got. Given this list, he's dropping off these bombs somewhere, and the first one is already there."

"Then that's where we put our resources first," said Jake. "You heard him . . . let's get this done. We've got to find this thing."

CHAPTER 23

After the room emptied, Jake and Mike were left alone. Jake turned to Mike.

"Do me a favor . . . get Sam Walsh on the phone, would you?" he said, staring at the information boards they had created.

"What's bothering you, Jake?"

He walked up to a board and pointed at HADJIALI.

"This . . . something about this . . . something bothers me."

Mike was already dialing as Jake spoke.

"Sam, Mike Lang. I'm putting you on speaker. Jake Sullivan's here."

"Sam, we've got a situation here."

"I know. The Bureau has called all of the analysts in. We're all working on it."

"Did you hear the latest?"

"The list?"

"Yeah," said Jake. "You have it there in front of you?"

"Just a second . . . it's coming in now. All right, I have it."

"See that language at the top? The HADJIALI?"

"Yeah."

"Do me a favor . . . I want you to do a little in-depth on that, would you? Work your magic. I think that means something more here than what everybody thinks it does. I think it's the key to this whole thing."

"I'll see if I can get away."

"If anybody gives you any trouble, have them call me. And another thing . . . how are you at analyzing photo cams and hacking the GPS on tractor trailers?"

There was a laugh on the other end of the line.

"What's bothering you?"

"The rest of this list . . . awful convenient this was sewn into the lining of a dead guy."

"You think it's a phony?"

"I don't know what to think just yet, but I'd sure like to know where in the hell that tractor trailer was really going."

"All right, Mr. Sullivan, I'm on it. I'll get back to you as soon as I can."

"Thanks, Sam. Make it quick. If this thing's real, Jacksonville and everywhere else is in a lot of trouble."

"Understood," and then the line went dead.

CHAPTER 24

Jake spent the rest of the day reallocating resources. Federal forces headed to Jacksonville, where the local police were briefed, and systematic raids were planned on cells the police had been investigating and keeping watch on. Random road checks were set up throughout the city and all tractor trailers were stopped.

The DEA was brought in and the word spread, purposely, that major drug take downs were underway. The idea was to keep panic from ensuing and keep the media at bay and in the dark.

In the interim, the police forces and political leaders of all cities on the list were brought up to date and resources were allocated to conduct similar raids and similar traffic stops in those areas.

The truck traffic on I-95 was voluminous, with over one hundred interstate trucking companies pinpointed by early evening.

Stops and raids in Jacksonville and points farther north on I-95 had produced nothing, and more were being planned for later, hopefully to turn up someone or something with knowledge that could be of help. As things stood, they had no further leads and some in their task force were more doubtful that the bombs had been loaded onto a tractor trailer.

Jake had gone home, wolfed down the dinner that Linda had prepared, told her as little as possible so she wouldn't worry, showered and grabbed a change of clothes and headed back to the office.

Fortunately, he had brought Mike with him, and there was something to smile about as they discussed news from Charlie Kosior and the Montezuma Treasure. The discussion also kept Linda from probing deeply into what was going on, although he could tell by the worry in her eyes that she knew it was something significant.

Mike also showered, changed into clothes he had brought with him to Jake's house, and they were now both back at the office going over the latest reports when the phone rang on Mike's desk.

"Mike Lang," he said. "Hold on . . . I'm putting you on speaker," and he looked at Jake. "It's Sam. He thinks he has something."

"What's up, Sam?" asked Jake.

"Oh, you know. Just working my magic, as usual. Sorry, not much of a time for levity . . . I understand," he said when he got no response.

"It's all right, Sam. What do you have?" asked Mike.

"Well, I'm not sure, and I don't know if it makes any sense, but here it goes:

I kept looking at the first part of that Arabic phrase . . . the 'HADJIALI' part . . . and believe it or not, I started thinking about something from when I was a kid . . . an old movie I watched. So I started checking movie databases, and I found it. It was a movie called *Southwest Passage* . . . originally made in 1954 . . . you know, one of those old movies . . . Rod Cameron and Joanne Dru. There was also a TV episode on the old *Death Valley Days* show in 1957 . . . I don't know where in the hell it was replayed, but that's where I saw it, and that's when I remembered the name."

"What are you talking about?" asked Mike.

"The name . . . that's what it is. 'HADJIALI' is a name."

Now Jake was interested.

"A name of who?"

"All right, listen . . . this is a really strange story, but you've got to listen. There was a guy named Hadji Ali who came to the United States. He was Syrian and Greek. He was also known as Philip Tedro, and he was also known as Hi Jolly."

"And?" said Jake.

"He was hired by the United States Army in the 1850's to create a corps of cavalry that would ride on camels in the southwestern desert. He was a breeder and a trainer. He started in 1856. The camel thing didn't work out and he started a freight service on the Colorado River. He worked with pack mules for the Army when they were hunting Geronimo, and in his final years, he moved to a place called Quartzsite, Arizona, and he was buried there, and there's a monument built to him. It's a little pyramid that's topped with a copper camel. And Quartzsite is outside of Phoenix, Arizona."

"So it's this guy's day of wrath?" asked Mike.

"Right," came the voice on the speaker.

Mike looked at Jake.

"It is Phoenix . . . it's the G8. G8 . . . eight bombs."

"We got anything to back this theory up?" asked Jake.

"That's the next thing I have to tell you," said Walsh. "I started looking at all that traffic cam footage. A lot of tractor trailers, so I jotted down the names. Then I searched traffic cams northbound out of Jacksonville. But in the midst of that, I came up with this Hi Jolly thing.

Quantico estimated time of death of Anwar as about 11:00 A.M., so I began checking traffic cam footage on I-95 from the nearest entrance ramp to the death scene northbound between 11:00 and 11:30, and I got seven hits. I then started looking for those same seven semis heading into Jacksonville and departing Jacksonville. I found four of the seven going in and three of the four going out before the road blocks were in place. That left one. At first I thought that was the one that was dropping its load off somewhere in Jacksonville that we had to find, but after what I found out about Arizona, I did some further checking . . . and I found the missing one. It's a 'Southern' truck. I zoomed it, and it's the same identification numbers as the one I saw on the I-95 ramp, almost adjacent to the crime scene."

"And where did you find it?" asked Mike.

"Heading west out of Jacksonville a couple of hours later, hopefully, after a meal or a nap, or, if we consider the worst, a drop off, on Interstate 10 . . . a direct route to Phoenix, Arizona, and Quartzsite . . . the burial place of Hadji Ali."

"Pretty confident about this, Sam?" asked Jake. "We're going to have to pull a lot of resources . . . piss off probably a lot of people . . . and we're basing it all on a dead camel driver."

"Well, I figured you might need better evidence, so I tried to hack the GPS on the truck, but it was disconnected."

"I know you, Sam," said Mike, "what's coming next?"

"Those trucks carry a black box that's wired independently."

"And you hacked it?" asked Jake.

"Let's just say the truck that you're looking for is sitting at a rest stop just off the Flora-Bama border."

"Sam," said Mike, "I never thought I'd say this, but it's an honor to know you."

"Great work, Sam," said Jake. "Great work."

"Let's just hope I'm right."

"I have a feeling you are," said Jake, "as a matter of fact, I'm going to bet everything I have on it. Now get off the line . . . I've got a lot of people to call."

"Go get 'em, guys," said Walsh, and his line went dead.

CHAPTER 25

The call from Luis to Havana was made over another long, complicated route.

"What is it?" came the Leader's voice.

"One of these geeks we have working for has been monitoring the truck. We think someone just hacked the black box."

"Impossible," came the voice, "how could they know?"

"I'm only telling you what he told me, boss."

"Goddamn Sullivan! All right . . . you know what to do. Move quickly. They'll have the local police there fast, followed by an army of Federales. Make sure our computer man is sent first . . . and make sure everything is disarmed on all further vehicles. Not doing it to the black box was a mistake!"

"I know," said Luis.

"There can be no more mistakes! Do you understand me?"

"Yes, Leader, I understand."

"Good. Then see to it."

Luis turned and used his encrypted phone to place a call to one of his operatives parked in a rest stop in Alabama.

"Get ready . . . we have a problem!"

CHAPTER 26

Luis stood over a computer operator, looking at a screen in the warehouse.

The truck was at a rest stop in Alabama, just across the Florida-Alabama border, and the **Southern** truck could be seen parked with its lights off. The camera feed was coming from a parked car, where the operative Luis had called was working a computer, disabling all the cameras at the rest stop facility. A message appeared on the screen: "Cameras disabled". Luis spoke into an encrypted phone.

"The cameras are down. Go. Now."

They watched as an old rusted customized van pulled up and parked beside the truck. When the van doors opened, however, they could see that everything had been removed from the interior, except the driver's seat. Using the small forklift, the eight crates were quickly offloaded from the truck and moved to the van, which was loaded by hand.

After everything had been replaced in the truck, the rear was locked and the driver took the passenger seat in the departing van.

Their operative working the camera remained and within only minutes after the offloading was completed, the area around the truck was swarming with flashing lights of the Alabama State Police.

They watched as they broke the lock of the back of the trailer and started rummaging through the boxes. They were soon joined by members of the FBI, Homeland Security, and other federal agencies.

Once again, Luis spoke into his phone.

"That's enough of the show. You sure no one is paying any attention to you?"

"They don't even know I'm here."

It was true, because after the van had left, he had exited his vehicle, taking his computer and camera with him, and was now amid the trees and the foliage on the other side of the rest area, nearest the highway.

After he finished speaking with Luis, a car, slowly and quietly, pulled onto the berm below the rest area and he quickly entered, and they drove off into the night.

Day 3

10/12

CHAPTER 27

"All right," said Jake, "enough!"

The angry back and forth between the members of the task force over the fiasco of the night before and how to determine the proper allocation of resources to combat the threat had carried over into accusations and where the blame should be placed for their failure so far to locate the nuclear weapons.

"You want to blame somebody," said Jake to the sudden quiet in the room, "blame me, but that doesn't solve our problem. What we need are new ideas. Now, does anybody have anything new that might help?"

"I might, Mr. Sullivan," said a voice from the back of the room.

Sam Walsh had slipped unnoticed into the conference room in the midst of the ongoing turmoil.

"Walsh, what are you doing here?" said Ted Forsythe of the FBI.

"Sorry, Mr. Forsythe, but this couldn't wait."

"It's all right, Ted," said Jake, "Sam's helped me out with some things. He's the one that tipped us off to the tractor trailer."

Forsythe sat back in his chair and stared at Jake.

"You don't like to go through channels, do you Sullivan? What the hell are you doing going around me on this and talking to my people?"

"We needed help and we needed it fast, and Sam here provided it."

Forsythe looked over at the analyst and sneered, "Yeah, a lot of good it did us."

Jake moved around the table until he was face-to-face with Forsythe.

"Listen, if you don't like the way I'm running this mission, you're free to leave. This isn't about protecting our own castles. This is about saving this country from a dire threat, and if you don't like the way I'm going about that, take it up with President Fletcher."

Forsythe stared long and hard at Jake and arose from his seat at the table.

"I'm done here." As he walked past Sam, heading for the door, he stopped. "Walsh, you just ruined your career. Your days at the FBI are done."

With that, he opened the door and exited, letting it slam behind him.

"Sam," said Jake, "take a seat. You're our new liaison with the FBI, and don't worry about your position. That's not going to be an issue. Anybody else have any problems they want to raise?"

The room was quiet.

"Now, lets' hear what this man has to say. Go ahead, Sam."

"First of all, we were right about the truck. Radiation tests showed radiation was at high level in places where the crates could have been located."

"Which means," said Ted Ristik of the CIA, "they had to be offloaded at the rest area before the police got there."

"Which means," said Mike, "that somehow they knew we were coming. They were tipped off."

Walsh lowered his head and stared at the table.

"I'm afraid that is on me."

"What do you mean?" said Jake.

"I went back and checked. These guys are way more sophisticated than I gave them credit for. I think they were able to determine that I hacked the black box. I checked the cameras at the rest stop. They were all remotely shut off right after I hacked into the truck. To do that, they would have to have had someone in the area with a laptop. They then would have had enough time to offload the crates into any other type of vehicle that would have room for them. I'm afraid I tipped them off."

"That's all right, Sam," Jake said as the room began to murmur again. "You're also the one that found them in the first place."

Bob Porter of Homeland Security then spoke up.

"Jake, I'm a little worried here. You seem to putting all our eggs in one basket, assuming that Mr. Walsh here is correct. What about everything we found out in the eight cities on that list? We found evidence in our raids in every city that there has been talk, at least on the street, of an eminent attack in each of those cities. We found a few documents . . . some recorded chatter. For all we know, they are still targets. Maybe there was something else radioactive on that truck . . . or maybe only one of the bombs . . . and the rest are still going to be used in seven of the eight cities on the east coast."

Mike looked over at him.

"Seems too good to be true, doesn't it? How often have you been able to obtain information like that? About terrorist attacks in eight separate cities . . . with information found in all of them?"

"You're saying it's planted?"

"I'm saying it seems too good to be true. What I'm saying is it could all be an elaborate deception, with the real target being the world leaders who are going to be at the G8 conference in Phoenix."

"What if you're wrong?" retorted Porter.

"That's the problem," interrupted Jake. "First we didn't have any leads, and now we have too many. As Sam said, these guys have a sophistication. They have skills. And I agree with Mike, I think they have too many skills to leave such an obvious trail. The black box of the truck heading out on I-10 was only found through Sam's diligence and abilities. What if they figured we were going to stay with the east coast scenarios and not look any further? And then there's this . . . tell them what else you found Sam, about the site in Arizona."

Walsh again went through the story of Hadji Ali and Quartzsite.

"You're telling me this whole plot has something to do with a camel driver in Arizona?" asked Porter.

"I can't tell you that, sir," said Walsh, "only that *Hadji Ali* are words that point to an individual who has a monument erected to him in a little town just outside Phoenix, Arizona, where the G8 conference is being held."

"It's not a coincidence," said Jake. "There's something there. I just can't put my finger on how it's going to play out, but there's something there."

Just then, Ristik's phone rang and he got up and walked to the back of the room, finished his conversation, and walked back to the group.

"You might be right, Jake. I think I've got another piece to the puzzle."

"Let's hear it."

"Our analysts have been checking financial transactions to see if there's any money going anywhere in this thing that might show us an ultimate destination. We've been looking at purchases, sales, everything you can think of . . . from offshore accounts we think might have some affiliation to al-Qaeda. We know they want to get back in the game. ISIS has stolen a lot of their thunder, and this is the type of move they'd make. Funny thing is, what we actually found doesn't have anything to do with al-Qaeda."

"What are you talking about?" asked Mike.

"There's a holding company called BM Holdings. We've been watching them for a while now. We noticed that just recently it's been selling off all of its properties along the California coast, and it has a ton of them. For a while, it was buying heavily all over the world, but the only thing it's been doing lately is selling those properties, and it's only purchased one other piece of land in the spring of this past year."

"Which is what?" asked Jake.

"A piece of desert just outside of Quartzsite, Arizona."

"But, you said it had no relationship to al-Qaeda," said Mike.

"No. This came up through our investigation of Group 45."

Mike looked at Jake.

"BM Holdings . . . Benjamin Matthews," muttered Jake. "Group 45 is directing this whole thing."

"Could be," said Ristik.

"That would explain the technical expertise," said Walsh.

"It could explain a lot of things," said Jake.

"We have another problem," said Ristik, "we're trying to connect it to this same company, but so far, we've had no luck."

"What was it?" asked Mike.

"I know DHS has been keeping this under the radar, but U.S. Customs and Border Protection have four MQ-9 Reaper drones stationed at Fort Huachuca, in Arizona, used for border patrol reconnaissance and seizures. Unfortunately, over the years, we've had some crashes of these drones, characterized, most frequently, as 'pilot error', in that this was being the operators on the ground."

Bob Porter stood up and slammed some paperwork on the desk.

"And that's all it was, damn it!"

Jake put up his hand for Porter to be quiet.

"Keep going, Ted. What's coming?"

"Up until last week, all the crashed drones were recovered."

"Why last week?" asked Mike.

"You want to tell them, Bob?" Ristik said to Porter.

Porter put his hands on his hips, hung his head, and stood there.

"C'mon Porter!" snapped Jake. "We don't have time for this! What's going on?"

"We had another drone crash . . . just across the border in Mexico."

"And . . .?" asked Jake.

"When we went to retrieve it, we couldn't find it."

"You lost a drone?" asked Mike.

Porter was silent.

"Problem is," said Ristik, "this thing easily has the ability to carry a suitcase-sized nuclear weapon."

Jake kept staring at Porter.

"Just the type of low-flying delivery system they'd want," said Jake.

"Look," said Porter, "there's no evidence whatsoever that this is involved in this in any way."

Jake turned and looked at Ristik.

"Anything show up anywhere?"

"No, but as soon as Rueben was done briefing us, I notified all agencies. Everyone is doing everything they can to locate the parts and/or what those parts might be reconstructed into."

"Shit!" said Mike, slumping into his chair.

"All right, here's what we're going to do," said Jake, and just then, the door opened, and in walked Ted Forsythe.

"My apologies to everyone," he said, looking around the room. "I received a call from the President a short while ago, who instructed me, rather clearly, as to my duty to him, to this group, and to this country. You were right, Jake, we're all in this together. Tell me what you need."

"Does your apology extend to Sam?" asked Jake.

"It does. Mr. Walsh, you did stellar work. The Bureau is proud of you. I don't think you have anything to worry about concerning your continued career."

"Thank you, Mr. Forsythe. I appreciate that," replied Walsh.

"Additionally, Jake, Mr. Walsh is at your service as long as this thing plays out."

"Apology accepted. All right, now," he said, looking at Porter, "everyone's ego better get the hell out of the equation! Understand? Now, let's get to work. We're going to divide this up.

We're going to keep working the eight cities on the coast, and Mike and I are going to form our own team and head out to Quartzsite, Arizona. Given what we know, and the puzzle certainly isn't complete, each of you let me know what men you think would be best to help us with what we're looking for, and we'll contact the locals in Phoenix and set up a command post.

Forsythe, Sam will bring you up to speed. Anything else?" Jake asked the group, but there were only nods of approval.

CHAPTER 28

Jake, Mike, Sam, and the rest of the team they had assembled flew by private jet to Phoenix that evening and landed at Sky Harbor Airport. They were loaded into the vehicles waiting for them in a private section of the airport and driven to the Executive Office Building in Phoenix to meet with the Governor, Thomas Sutton.

The Governor's office and conference room were on the ninth floor of the Executive Office Building, in that Arizona did not maintain a Governor's mansion for their chief executive, who resided in his own residence during his term of office.

Every effort had been made to keep their arrival under wraps, and Jake was pleased to see that there was no news media present when they pulled into the garage, got out, and took elevators to the ninth floor.

As soon as Jake entered the room, he moved to the Governor, thanked him for his hospitality, and extended his hand.

"Governor Sutton, thank you for your prompt assembling of this group and allowing us to set up shop here."

"We're glad to have you, Mr. Sullivan. Your reputation and the reputation of Mr. Lang certainly precede you. You and these fine people you brought with you to help protect our state are greatly appreciated."

There were several other people in the room, and as Jake and his staff took their seats, the Governor introduced the six other individuals in the room.

"This is Hector Alfonso, my Chief of Staff, Thomas Garrison, the Head of the Arizona State Police, whom I believe you know, Edward Falcon, our liaison with Homeland Security, Malcolm Dahl, SAC of the Phoenix FBI, and Philip Winters, the Commander of our Border Patrol Units here in Arizona."

The Governor then motioned to a young lady sitting at the end of the table.

"And this young lady is Miss Chestine Harris, an instructor and holder of the Chair in Geology at Arizona State University, and someone who knows the area around Quartzsite probably better than anyone else in this state. Mr. Sullivan, you have the floor."

"Thank you all for being here. Hopefully, the advance team we sent out has briefed you on everything we know so far about the situation. We have concluded that Quartzsite, Arizona, has something to do with a planned nuclear attack on the United States. We believe it also has something to do with the G8 Conference in Phoenix that begins in three days.

It is our belief, and we have no hard evidence at the present time to support this belief, that there's more to this than just an attack on the G8. We believe eight suitcase-sized nuclear weapons were smuggled into the United States through the Port of Miami on the 9th of October. Eight *nuclear* weapons," Jake emphasized. "Which is one of the reasons we think there's more to this plan. In the documents you were provided, we received a list of eight cities on the east coast, which we originally thought were potential targets, and they still may be, but we also tend to believe that list was planted and was a diversion, and the real attacks are going to occur here in your state. The only other new information we've obtained was that Group 45 might be involved in this whole matter, allying itself with al-Qaeda."

The head of the State Police, Colonel Thomas Garrison, spoke up.

"And the information that supports that is that you believe they've sold off a lot of property on the California coast, and," he said, staring at Winters, "they may have gotten their hands on a drone?"

"That's right," said Jake. "We don't know the connection yet, although we fear that the drone may be used as a low altitude delivery system for a nuclear weapon over the City of Phoenix."

"Excuse me," came a quiet voice from the end of the table.

"Yes . . . Miss Harris, is it?"

"Yes. Thank you, Mr. Sullivan. I also see that this same company that sold off its property on the California coast also bought a patch of desert south of Quartzsite."

"That appears to be true, yes."

"This afternoon after we received your briefing papers, I drove out there. There's nothing there. No buildings, no tracks of vehicles, no anything. It's the site of the old Chocolate Mountain Gold Mine and Stamp Mill."

"Again, it appears to be a piece of a larger puzzle, but we aren't sure how it fits," said Mike. "It could be another diversion. Group 45 is very sophisticated. We've found them to be very adaptive to diversionary tactics. That's why we can't take any chances. We can only go with what we know and what we believe to be the case at the moment, and we appreciate the help of all of you to find any more information you can, or give us anything you can, so that we can zero in and stop this."

"Understood, Mr. Lang," said the Governor. "Any questions from anybody? My team is here to assist you, gentlemen," and he got up and shook hands with Jake. "I'll leave you to it. If there is anything else you need from me, just let me know."

"Thank you, Governor, I appreciate everything," said Jake.

After the Governor departed, the group began to plan for what the morning might bring.

"I'll tell you, Mr. Sullivan," said Colonel Garrison, "I'm glad it's not January or February. If it was, we'd have thousands of RVs to search. There's still a lot of them out here. It's going to take a lot of man power to check them all in the time we have. Naturally, we'll put up road blocks where necessary and check everybody coming in, but if somebody is already here, it's going to be like looking for a needle in a haystack."

"I understand, Colonel. We'll give you as much federal man power as you need, but it's just something we have to do. An RV could have easily been converted to fit these eight crates."

"I understand," said Garrison, "and that's what worries me. We'll get on it right away, and I promise you, we'll do our best."

"I have no doubt, Colonel. Thank you," said Jake.

Just then, Chestine Harris was leaving the room and Jake stopped her.

"Miss Harris . . . I wonder if you'd be so kind to take Mike and me out to Quartzsite tomorrow? I'd like to look around and see if I can figure out the connection."

"I have to admit, Mr. Sullivan, your suspicions are based on pretty tenuous data."

"That doesn't matter," said Mike, "trust me . . . he feels it in his gut . . . and his gut's usually right."

Chestine laughed and looked at Jake.

"Is that true, Mr. Sullivan?"

"Sort of," he said. "I do get feelings about things. Sometimes they pan out . . . and please, call me Jake . . . and you can call this guy Mike."

She laughed, "Thank you, Jake . . . and Mike."

"I have to admit," said Mike, "I'm thinking about this like you are. I just can't see what this patch of desert out in the middle of nowhere is going to have to do with all of this . . . but . . . like I said, he hasn't been wrong too often."

"I think Quartzsite might surprise you, Mike, especially when I take you to the Quartzsite Yacht Club."

"There's a yacht club . . ." asked Mike, "in the middle of the desert . . . where there's no water . . .?"

"I told you you'd be surprised. When and where do you gentlemen want me to pick you up?"

"We're staying at the Hilton. About 8:00 A.M.?" said Jake.

"Sounds like a plan," she said. "I'll see you then," and off she went.

Jake gathered his things and walked over to Mike.

"Come on. Let's get a ride back to the hotel. We'll make some plans for tomorrow."

"Plans? Jake . . . we're going to a yacht club in the middle of the desert . . . and you want to make plans?"

Jake walked out in front of him.

"Mike, sometimes you amaze me at your lack of imagination."

"Yeah," said Mike, as he followed, "but I'm well-grounded in reality, which is more than I can say for some other people."

Day 4

10/13

CHAPTER 29

Jake and Mike were up and showered, had eaten breakfast, and were waiting outside when Chestine pulled up and picked them up in front of the Hilton at 8:00 A.M., sharp.

She headed through the city center and got on the westbound ramp heading out on I-10 towards the California border. It was a bright, sunny day with clear blue skies, and it was growing hot already.

"Quartzsite is about one hundred fifty miles from here," she said, "but I-10 is a straight shot, so going seventy miles per hour is no problem," and she kept that pace until she had to slow down for a road block set up by the State Police about ten miles outside of Quartzsite, that cost them about a half an hour, but they still arrived before 11:00 A.M.

CHAPTER 30

Mike got out and stretched and looked around, having been in the back seat of the Jeep.

As they had come into town, sporadic buildings appeared along the sides of the highway clustered around the intersection of I-10 and I-95, and then began to thin out again as I-10 went further west. From behind the buildings the desert spread out as far as the eye could see, RVs parked throughout.

In talking with Jake about what they were going to do once they arrived, Mike had looked over maps and realized that the town of Quartzsite sat in the western portion of what was called the LaPosa Plain, along the Tyson Wash. The Dome Rock Mountains were off to the west, and the California border. The Granite Mountains were to the southwest and the Plomosa Mountains to the east from where they had come.

Taking it all in, he turned and looked at Chestine.

"So, this is it, huh?"

"Welcome to Quartzsite, Mike."

"So where do we start?" asked Jake.

"We are going to meet MeMe Selleck."

"And who might that be?" asked Jake.

"She's the owner and operator of the Quartzsite Yacht Club that I told you about," and she pointed about fifty yards down the highway, where the sign for the club was bathed in mid-day sunlight.

CHAPTER 31

They walked into a door under the sign and a young lady with dark hair behind the bar turned around and screamed, "Chestine!" and sped over to embrace her in a warm hug.

"Hi MeMe. How have you been?"

"Oh, you know . . . getting everything back into shape. We just opened last week. Getting ready for the season."

"The season?" asked Mike.

MeMe looked around Chestine at the two gentlemen and back at Chestine with questions in her eyes.

"Pardon my manners. MeMe Selleck . . . this is Jake Sullivan and Mike Lang. They'd like to talk to you if they might."

"About what?" said MeMe to Chestine in a soft voice.

"I think it's better if they explain it. Can we sit down somewhere for a little while?"

She looked around.

"Yeah, the lunch crowd hasn't gotten here yet. When they do, I'm going to have to leave. I'm short-staffed today."

Jake walked over and extended his hand.

"Thank you for meeting with us, Ms. Selleck. We'll take as little of your time as possible."

She pointed to a large table with several chairs over in the corner.

"We'll sit over there. You boys look like you could use something to eat. Today's special is a Southwest burger . . . fries on the side."

"Her food is really good," said Chestine.

"I'm sold," said Mike. "I'll take one. Cold, cold water if you have it."

"Same for me," said Jake.

"Me, too," said Chestine, "why not?"

"Let me get this started and then I'll come over and we can talk."

When MeMe arrived at the table, Jake and Mike began to explain the situation with as little detail as they could. They were interrupted by the serving of their lunch and took time to eat.

"Delicious," Mike said.

"I agree," said Jake.

"Well, we aim to please. Glad you like it," said MeMe. "So what exactly do you need from me?"

"Well, we are interested in any strangers that might have arrived in the last couple of days . . . anything you might have seen that seems out of the ordinary . . . anything suspicious."

MeMe rested her chin on her hands, elbows on the table, and looked off into space. Just as she did, a big man in dusty overalls entered the restaurant and took a seat at the bar. MeMe pointed.

"He got here last night," she said. "He's staying over at the motel. Said his name's Joe. He's on his way to California but wanted to look around the old mines in the area."

"Do you know what kind of vehicle he has?" asked Mike.

"Yeah, it's one of those customized vans . . . pretty dirty and beat up. It's parked out in front of the motel."

"Colonel Garrison of the State Police mentioned something to us," said Mike, "that in January and February there are thousands of RVs around here. What goes on?"

"Quartzsite's nickname is 'the Rock Capital of the World'. This town, like everything else around here, came into existence because of mining . . . gold, silver, quartz . . . anything you can think of. People come out here to mineral shows, swap meets . . . it's a big flat area where people can park their RVs and have a good time, and that's what they do . . . it becomes a celebration."

"So there are a lot of mines around here?" asked Jake.

"Hah, you have no idea," said MeMe. "People like Chestine, along with the Bureau of Land Management, have been trying to close them. They are a real danger. You could be walking along and step right into a shaft."

"I'm going to take them out to the old Chocolate Mine and Stamp Mill," said Chestine. "You hear about anything going on out there?"

"Nope," said MeMe.

More people were coming in, and MeMe stood up.

"Look, sorry I couldn't give you much help, but I've got to get to work. The crowd is starting to come in."

"We understand," said Jake, standing up and again shaking her hand. "We appreciate everything, and please give us a bill for lunch."

"No, that's no problem. It's on me. Chestine here is an old friend, and if you're her friends, you've got to be good people . . . even if you are with the federal government."

Jake laughed.

"Well, thank you again for your time . . . and if you see or hear anything . . ."

"Don't worry, I'll be in touch."

"Here's my card, just in case," said Jake.

"And mine, too," said Mike. "Call if you come up with anything. But, before you go, I've got to ask you something."

"What's that?" asked MeMe.

"The yacht club thing . . . in the desert? How'd this happen?"

"I'll give you the short version," said MeMe. "A guy named Al Madden had an investment company in California, and in the 70's he came out here working on a gold mine venture for some clients. He spent a lot of time here and noticed that the local beer bar called 'The Jigsaw' was for sale, and he bought it. Al looked around and realized he was in the middle of the desert, an ocean of desert, and he decided to have a little fun. Renamed the bar the Yacht Club, and his motto was 'Welcome aboard – long time no sea.' Al sold memberships to the yacht club to anyone that came in the door. All you needed was ten dollars – that's gone up to forty – but that's still all you need. Now we have over ten thousand members from all over the world, and it is *the* biggest yacht club on the planet. And you know one of the great things about yacht clubs, don't you?"

"No, not really," said Mike. "What's that?"

"Reciprocity. People have come in here and have told us they have shown their cards at yacht clubs all over the world and then gotten in. So, that's the story of this little place, and now, I've got to get to work."

"Thanks, MeMe," said Mike. "Appreciate everything . . . your help, the food, and the story."

"My pleasure. See you later, Chestine."

"Bye, MeMe. Now that you've learned the history of the Quartzsite Yacht Club, want to head out to the old mine and snoop around?"

"Lead the way," said Jake, and they got up and headed back to the Jeep.

CHAPTER 32

As they headed back to the Jeep, they walked past the motel and easily spotted the van that MeMe had talked about. The side windows of the driver and front passenger doors were darkened, as were the two porthole windows in the body of the van, not uncommon in the desert to keep out the heat. Looking through the front window didn't help, as there was a curtain drawn across the interior.

Mike circled the van, stopping now and again to squat down, looking at the tire and the undercarriage of the vehicle. He got up and looked at Jake.

"What's bothering you, Mike?"

"It just seems funny to me. This van doesn't particularly look like it's been taken care of, but it has four new tires and four new extra duty shocks. Doesn't seem to fit with the overall décor. I think we should have a little conversation with Joe, the new visitor."

"Why don't you go to the Jeep, Chestine, and get the air conditioner running? Mike and I will walk back and see if we can have a little chat with this guy. You can pull down and pick us up there if you want to."

"Will do," she said and headed toward the Jeep.

Jake and Mike made their way back to the restaurant and walked in. The bar stool where Joe had been sitting was now occupied by a young guy in a t-shirt and baseball cap. Mike walked over to MeMe, who was now behind the bar.

"You guys back already?"

"Joe, that you mentioned . . . when did he leave?"

"Right after you guys did. He cancelled his order and headed out the door."

Jake and Mike once again exchanged glances.

"That number on the card that I gave you, MeMe, you can reach me on that, anytime. If he comes back in, give me a call."

"Sure. What's the problem with Joe?"

"May not be anything," said Mike, "we just need to talk to him."

"Okay, you've got it," and MeMe was off to another customer. "Hey, Harry . . . how's it going? Find any new rocks?"

CHAPTER 33

When Jake and Mike went outside, Chestine was waiting for them, and they got in the Jeep. As they pulled off, Joe came around the corner of the Yacht Club and then headed in the opposite direction, past several store fronts to a parking lot that housed used cars and quickly found the pickup truck where he was told it would be. The driver's side door was unlocked and the keys were under the mat. He pulled out and headed south into the desert. Along the way, he pulled out his encrypted phone and made a call.

"They're here. Yeah, I recognized them right away. They have some girl with them. I think they were pressing the owner of the Yacht Club for some information. I noticed they all looked my way when I came in and sat down, then I saw them looking around the van. I think they're suspicious."

The voice at the other end was furious.

"Damn Sullivan and Lang! How did they figure this out? Get out there and watch them! Can they do anything?"

"No. They don't have the equipment."

"Then you know what to do when they're gone. Just like we talked about," came the voice over the phone.

"You want me to take care of this particular problem?"

"Luis will be in touch with you later. Just watch them for now . . . and make sure our cargo is protected. Luis will be in touch."

"Understood."

Joe was ex-Marine – tough . . . battle-hardened . . . by two tours in Afghanistan . . . but he was also fed up. He also had lost faith in his government . . . a government that he believed didn't care about the men that bled and died in the far parts of the world in places where victory would never be achieved, and the wars would go on and on. He was an easy recruit for Group 45.

CHAPTER 34

As Chestine's Jeep was bouncing along the semblance of a road that headed out into the southern desert, Jake's encrypted phone rang. It was Jason Bates, President Fletcher's Chief of Staff.

Blunt as always, he barked, "Anything to report?"

"More pieces of the puzzle, Jason, but nothing definitive."

"We're running out of time."

"Think there's any chance of getting the President to continue or cancel the G8?"

"None," came the reply. "You know how he is. He's not going to let these people scare him off."

"So what's the current plan?"

"The other leaders are in or coming in throughout today and tomorrow . . . reception at the White House tomorrow night . . . wheels up at 7:00 A.M. on the fifteenth . . . should touch down in Phoenix at 8:30 your time at Sky Harbor . . . opening ceremonies at 8:00 P.M."

"Doesn't give us a hell of a lot of time."

"It's all you have."

"I know," said Jake.

"You two guys get to work. Keep me posted," leaving Jake to just look at the phone, as Bates was gone.

"So, is old Jason as happy as usual?" asked Mike.

"You could say that," said Jake, "you could say that."

CHAPTER 35

As Jake and company were nearing the remnants of the Chocolate Mountain Mine and Stamp Mill, a phone was ringing in a vehicle that was on its way to Quartzsite from Phoenix. Luis answered the man he knew as the Leader and knew the call had originated in Havana and pinged on towers all over the world before it got to his phone. The Leader was furious, as Luis spoke to him.

"Yes, I met with him last night and gave him his instructions. How did Sullivan find out?"

"Luis, we cannot change our plans! They must be eliminated! I personally instructed our asset to move our cargo today, and tonight, you are to instruct him to take out Sullivan and Lang."

"What about the girl you mentioned?" asked Luis.

"Collateral damage. She is of no importance to me . . . one way or the other. Make sure our asset doesn't fail."

"Do you want me to stay and help?"

"No. It is imperative that you go to the site. Do we have any problems there?"

"No. Our men our mingling in with the few tourists that showed up. No sign of any activity. It appears Sullivan and Lang are focusing on that shithole of a town in the middle of the desert and don't know about the ultimate site for deployment."

"We must keep it that way, Luis. Understood?"

"Absolutely, sir," he replied.

"And our Arab fanatics are prepared?"

"They are being kept in one of our houses across the border in California. They'll arrive tonight along with their drivers and we will give them their destinations. They'll leave and take the rest of the night and tomorrow to get in place."

"Ah, yes . . . get in place for al-Qaeda's glorious moment . . . on the feast of Eid-al-Fitr . . . and cause the economic and social chaos that will ensue and the complete destruction of all faith in the United States government. The people we have in place will be able to take over quite easily. And then, my friend, we will be in charge . . . which reminds me . . . one last thing, Luis . . . the drone?"

"The parts arrived throughout the week, most coming in as scrap metal. The tech people put everything together in a lab across the California border. Final assembly occurred just off-site, and a helicopter lifted it into position. All that remains is the programming, which I personally will take care of. The world's focus will be on Phoenix . . . or what's left of it . . . and our mission in California will go unnoticed until it's too late."

"Excellent! Excellent!" said the Leader. "And I am ensured that the money that we have accumulated from the sale of our California properties has been timed for distribution to the proper people, just as the chaos erupts, and they will ensure that matters proceed. First a call for martial law, then a suspension of habeas corpus, and one-by-one, they will gain control of the government . . . and we will be in power. That is why we must not fail, Luis. This is the moment that Group 45 has planned for since its inception. We must not fail."

"Understood, Leader. I am honored you have selected me to be in charge."

"Honored you should be," said the Leader, "but you know the price if you fail."

"Something I accept, sir."

"Something over which you have no choice, my friend."

And with that, he was gone.

CHAPTER 36

"You'll see the derricks coming up soon," said Chestine. "We're just south of Q Mountain. It'll be up on those slopes to your left," she said, pointing out her open window, as she turned the Jeep in that direction.

Slowly, the wheels and gears of the derrick that sat over the shaft came into view, as well as dilapidated wooden buildings sitting on the slope of a hillside, the desert sun glaring down on top of them.

Chestine stopped the car and they exited, their view hazy with the heat shimmering, as if they were approaching a desert oasis, but this was not the stuff of palm trees and watering holes in the middle of the desert. These were the remnants of what once was – a throwback to the late Nineteenth Century and the history of this southwest corner of the United States. While everyone recalls the romantic vision of the gun fight at the OK Corral between the Earps and the Clantons, few realize that Tombstone was just another mining town, one of many scattered throughout the desert. It grew and shrank in a certain rhythm with the minerals that were extracted from the earth.

"Doesn't look like anyone's home," said Jake.

"I'm not so sure about that," said Mike, walking around the derrick. "These tire tracks sure as hell look like they'd match that van.

And look at this cable going down to the shaft. See where this ends, clamped to the piling? These bolts are new."

"And these tracks weren't here when I was out here," said Chestine.

Jake stepped over to the edge of the shaft to look down.

"Probably deep enough to hide a couple packages, don't you think?"

"You think the nukes are in there?" asked Chestine.

"Look at it this way," said Mike, "if you came out here and looked around, not knowing what we know, you wouldn't notice anything odd out here."

Jake took out his encrypted phone and called one of the team back in Phoenix.

"Listen, we think we've found something. We're staring down a deep well shaft of an old mine site. Ping my location on the phone. Get a team out here with a hoist, wench, and anything you need to haul up whatever's down there. We might have found what we're looking for . . . yeah . . . radioactive gear. How long? Get a drone up and put eyes on this. We're going to move out of here. If somebody other than us comes by for this, we'll know and we can track them. All right, put him on."

Jake looked at Mike.

"Sam has something for us. Yeah, Sam, what is it? Chestine, write this down, will you?" asked Jake. "Go ahead, Sam, you're on speaker."

"Jake, we've just picked up some new chatter and I wanted to get it to you."

"What's the translation?"

"We don't have any idea what it means yet, but we're working on it. Here it is: 'Peace be with you. We are at Peace. The Wrath awaits.' Then all we can make out is a series of what appears to be random letters. I'm running them through every cypher I can think of to see what they mean, but here it is: 'DHSSBPFPDCPRSBB'."

Chestine showed what she had written to Mike, who looked at her and shook his head.

Turning the phone off speaker, Jake spoke, "All right, thanks Sam. Get on it. It's important. What? Tell him to pull his men and get out here! Yeah . . . now! All right, good."

Jake turned off his encrypted phone and just shook his head.

"What's up?" asked Mike.

"Garrison's worried about leaving the road blocks to get out here and take care of this. Said it's going to take a while to pull everybody in. You heard what I said."

"What's with this new code?"

"I don't know," Chestine replied. "I just don't know."

"Well, Sam's going to work on it. Hopefully, he'll be able to give us some answers," said Jake.

"Until then, let's get back to Quartzsite. Chestine, do you think MeMe would mind letting us set up a command post at her restaurant? I want to stay on top of this and stay as close as we can to this situation."

"I'll talk to her, Jake. I don't think it will be a problem."

"Good. Let's head back. That drone should be in the sky . . . and we'll see how this plays out."

Joe had driven in a wide loop around the mine site, staying in the low washes that ran through the area, going slow so as not to raise a cloud of dust, and staying out of the direct line of site from the mine, until he found a spot to park that he had scouted earlier that morning and made his way to higher ground so he was looking down on the abandoned site. He checked his angle with the sun to make sure there would be no reflection off his binoculars as he watched Jake, Mike, and Chestine examine the cable he had placed and saw them looking down into the shaft.

"Not bad, boys . . . not bad," he mumbled to himself. He knew that it wasn't going to do them any good, as he saw them walk down the slope, get in the Jeep, and head back to Quartzsite. *"Now, if they know . . . why'd they leave? Why not stay and protect the goods?"* He then looked up into the clear sky and laughed to himself. *"Same old shit. You're going to wait for me to do the work and then follow me, huh? We'll see."*

And with that, he took out his computer and entered several lines of code.

"That should make you blind for all the time I need," he again said to himself, as he headed down the slope towards the pickup.

CHAPTER 37

Back in Phoenix, the tech specialist was sitting at his computer, watching the ground, as the drone he had sent out flew over the desert of Arizona, almost ready to hone in on the site that Jake had provided through the coordinates on his phone, when his screen went dark. Frantically he entered code after code and then shut it down and re-booted, but nothing.

"We've lost image!" he yelled, and his superior hurried over.

"Get out of there . . . let me in there," and he took over the seat, and he too entered code after code and finally sat back, looking at the dark screen. "What the hell just happened?" he asked. "Call the team that's headed out there and tell them to move their asses. We don't have eyes anymore."

Joe pulled up the pickup truck next to the mine shaft and maneuvered it so the back was close to the edge. He then removed the snap-on bed cover and began fitting the pipes into place with the equipment the truck had been fitted with. He had to admit . . . these guys he worked for were good, making sure there was a backup at all times . . . this truck being his.

He quickly set up the hoist and wench, plugged it into the truck's power system, and started it. The cable slowly started to rise up from the mine. Soon the first canvas backpack came into view. He unhooked it and secured it in the truck bed and did so for seven more. He worked steadily and with no great urgency. He knew how long it would take someone to get out there, and he knew he'd be done before they arrived.

When all eight backpacks were secure, he dismantled the equipment and stowed it in the truck and snapped back on the cover. Before he got in, he took out a change of clothes and removed the fake beard and mop of hair from his head, revealing a blondish buzz-cut. He used a canteen to wash the stickum off his face, and when he was done, he packed everything into an extra bag he had, found what he believed to be a sufficiently heavy rock, put it in, and threw everything into the bottom of the shaft, along with the cable that he had been using.

Whistling, he put on an Arizona Diamondbacks cap and hopped into the truck and took another road back to Quartzsite, parking the vehicle in the shade of a building and making sure it was locked.

He then crossed a small stretch of desert and entered an RV, turned on the power, turned up the air conditioning, made sure it kicked in, and took a cold bottle of beer out of the refrigerator, took a couple swigs, and lay down to get some sleep before he had to commence his night's work.

CHAPTER 38

On the way back to the Yacht Club, Chestine pulled over and stopped at a side road.

"You've come all this way," she said. "You need to see this," and she exited the Jeep.

Jake and Mike got out and followed her. She led them into the Quartzsite Cemetery and stopped at a stone pyramid topped with a copper camel.

"This was established in 1935 by then Governor Benjamin Moeur. This is the grave of Hadji Ali."

"I get the irony," said Jake. "He came here from the Middle East and he became a 'faithful aid to the U.S. Government'."

"So this 'Wrath' that they want to create is for this guy?" asked Mike.

"More like a comeuppance," said Chestine. "The story of Hi Jolly covers a lot of ground. Supposedly he was in California trying to become a part of something there, but because of who and what he was, the upper class would have none of it, so at one of their famous social events, he supposedly sent his camels running through. Not a good metaphor, but you get the idea."

"Take it to the ruling class," said Jake. "Some things never change. You're sure everything is okay with MeMe?"

"Sure, you heard my phone call. She's glad to help. We can get over there and get started."

"When we get there, I'll call Sam," Jake said to Mike. "Maybe he'll have some more on that new code he found."

CHAPTER 39

Meme had cleared space around the corner table, where there were several State Troopers standing.

"What's going on?" asked Jake. "Why aren't you guys headed out to the mine?"

"Tactical team already left, Mr. Sullivan. We're back here checking computers, seeing if we can get the drone back online."

"What?! What are you talking about?" asked Mike.

"Drone camera went out for about forty-five minutes. Then it came back on. We're trying to see if we can pull film."

"Was Garrison and his crew out there, then?"

"No, they wouldn't have gotten out there 'til after that, Mr. Sullivan."

"Why the hell not?" asked Jake. "I told him to get out there as fast as they could."

"The Colonel said it took time to get people in place. That's all I can tell you. Hold on Mr. Sullivan. The boss is on the line now. Here . . ." and he handed Jake the phone.

"Colonel, what the hell is going on?!"

"I was going to ask you the same thing, Sullivan. I don't know why the hell you made us hurry up and get the hell out here. There's nothing here."

"Did you take the equipment to pull that cable up?"

"There is no cable. There's nothing here."

"Give me that," said Mike, hearing the Colonel talk over speaker. "Colonel, this is Mike Lang. Look on the bottom right of that gantry. Are there new screws there?"

"Hold on . . . I'm looking . . . no, there's nothing here."

"What about fresh holes?"

"Possible. No metal. No cable."

"Can you get a guy down that shaft?" asked Mike.

"Lang, you've seen this. No way a man could fit down there."

"Can you send down a camera?" asked Mike.

There was silence for a minute.

"Yeah, we should be able to do that. Put me back on the line with one of my men. I'll get it out here."

Mike thrust the phone back at the trooper, who went off to talk to the Colonel. Jake sat down hard in a chair and slammed his fist on the table.

"My Goddamn fault! We never should have left!" and he looked up at Mike.

"You know they took out that drone . . . and you know they came and got the nukes out of that hole."

Jake shook his head in agreement and said, "Pretty good bet . . . and we have no idea where they are going."

"You saw the van was still there, right?"

"Yeah, they switched vehicles . . . if it was him."

"Let's go take a look anyway. We'll see what we can find. It might even give us a lead."

Jake got up, tired and angry.

"Don't count on it," he said, "I'm not."

CHAPTER 40

Just as they were ready to leave, Chestine came up to them.

"Jake . . . Mike . . . can I have a minute?"

"What is it, Chestine?" asked Jake, his tone harsh.

"I'm sorry . . . I just wanted to run something by you, a thought that I had."

"Don't pay any attention to him. Go ahead," said Mike. "What have you got?"

"As part of the geology courses that we teach at Arizona State, we do a lot of in-field work with the various fault lines that pass through Arizona, and we also do a lot of work monitoring mining sites in this state. We work in conjunction with the Bureau of Land Management, closing abandoned mines. When Arizona was first settled, mining was its major occupation, as I told you. One of the biggest mining towns was named La Paz. It was a gold mining town along the Colorado River, close to the California border. At one time, it was the largest town in the territory, and in 1863 it was considered for the Arizona territorial capital, but like all other mining towns, the gold was depleted and everyone moved on, and it became a ghost town. The only town left there now is stone ruins, the foundations of old buildings."

Suddenly she stopped. She could see that she was losing them.

"I'm sorry. I'm getting off the point. The real point of all this is that in studying the fault lines and the mine systems and the desert to the west of here, it got me interested in studying faults and the movement of the plates under the earth in general. Given our location, I've become fascinated with one of the most famous faults there is."

"The San Andreas?" asked Mike.

"Exactly!" she said excitedly.

"I'm sorry," said Jake, "but I'm not following this. What does the San Andreas Fault have to do with us?"

"Let me explain. You have to understand the San Andreas Fault is a boundary that slides between the Pacific plate and the North American plate, and it slices California in two from the northern part of the state to the Mexican border. Because of my interest in it, I started reading everything I could find about it, and I came across a paper. It was submitted to one of our national publications by a group of geologists, and the thesis was whether or not the detonation of a nuclear weapon could affect the fault."

Jake looked at Mike.

"And you think . . ."

"Wait, please, Jake . . . let me finish. The basic view of the geologists who wrote that paper was that a singular nuclear weapon would not be powerful enough to have a major impact, although if it hit precisely at a point directly on the fault line where there has been great variability in the past, it might cause localized damage . . . perhaps even a significant earthquake in the actual area of the blast."

"And?" said Mike.

"Those types of variable areas are in communities that lie directly on the fault line. If you start in the south, there's Desert Hot Springs, then San Bernardino, Palmdale, Frazier Park, Daly City just outside of San Francisco, Point Reyes Station, and Bodega Bay."

"You just named seven cities," said Jake, looking at Mike.

"I know," she said. "What if . . . just what if . . . Quartzsite isn't going to be the site of the entire attack, but there is a planned drone strike on the G8 meeting in Phoenix . . . that leaves seven nuclear bombs. If you calculate the potential blast force of those bombs, all set off at the same time on the seven variable fault sites I mentioned, you could have the most significant earthquake and tsunami in the history of mankind, let alone the effects of the nuclear blast, which would absolutely destroy the entire coast of California."

"Then what's the significance of Quartzsite?" asked Mike.

"It's the perfect hiding place. If you have studied the area, you could store nuclear bombs in any of the mine shafts all over the area. It would simply be pickup and delivery, and then the bombs could be transported to the seven blast sites. And there is one more thing," she said, and she showed them her notepad, on which was written the following:

<u>D</u>esert <u>H</u>ot <u>S</u>prings

<u>S</u>anta <u>B</u>arbara

<u>P</u>almdale

<u>F</u>razier <u>P</u>ark

<u>D</u>aly <u>C</u>ity

<u>P</u>oint <u>R</u>eyes <u>S</u>tation

<u>B</u>odega <u>B</u>ay

"It's the code that Sam gave us."

"You're right," said Jake. "That's why they sold off all their property on the California coast. They're going to attack the G8, but that's not the major portion of their plan. This is."

"Remember, this is just a theory I have."

"Yeah," said Jake, "but it's a theory that makes sense and answers a lot of questions we had. It explains the number of weapons that are in play. It explains the code. It explains everything."

"And," added Mike, "it fits into the whole purpose for being of Group 45. Not even considering the loss of life and the devastation this would cause, it would cripple the United States economy for years, decimate our Pacific defenses, and possibly destroy the government."

"Wait a minute," said Jake, "what about the rest of the message . . . Peace be with you . . . We are at peace . . . The Wrath awaits?"

Chestine looked at him and smiled.

"You know, don't you?"

"I just told you about La Paz . . ."

"Peace," said Mike. "It's Spanish for peace. We are at Peace."

Jake looked at him.

"The Wrath awaits . . . La Paz is the distribution point. It's not Quartzsite. They were just using this place to hide the bombs."

"I think so," said Chestine.

Jake looked at Mike.

"I know so," and Mike nodded his head and said, "If they've got to move these things up and down the California coast, distribution is going to happen tonight."

CHAPTER 41

Jake and Mike had a video conference session with all of the members of the team using the space provided to them by MeMe at the Yacht Club for their base of operations.

They had broken into Joe's van and the back had clearly been modified to carry cargo, and they were more sure than ever that he was their man. APBs had been put out but there had been no sighting of Joe anywhere.

More tactical units were on their way to La Paz, coming from both California to the west and Phoenix to the east, and they were forming a broad circle around the ruins that constituted the one time mining town, staying well out of sight. Helicopters were prepped to take off from the proving grounds at Yuma, and all conceivable avenues that would lead into La Paz were cut off except one – the direct route on I-10, which is the way everyone presumed people would be moved in and out, and they wanted to make sure that everyone would arrive and be swept up in the same net.

There still had been nothing found on the east coast, and Jake and Mike were more certain than ever that they were correct, based upon the information provided them by Chestine, the code, and their own discoveries.

CHAPTER 42

Colonel Garrison had come back as the session had started, mildly complaining of being sent on a wild goose chase out to the mine site, making sure that he let everyone know his belief that Mike and Jake were wrong in their assessment.

"That's the craziest bullshit I've ever heard," he said, "blow up the San Andreas Fault and knock California into the Goddamn ocean. Aside from being every right-winger's dream, that's just plain old crap."

Mike stared at him, anger in his eyes.

"Thanks for the input, Colonel. Duly noted. Now, if you don't mind, we've got work to do."

"Go ahead . . . chase your fairytale, but my men aren't going to be a part of it."

Now it was Jake's turn.

"Sorry, Colonel, your Governor signed on. He agrees. So, you're going to do exactly what we tell you to do. Understood?"

The Colonel just glared and walked away.

Just then, a call came in. It was Sam Walsh.

"It's Jake, Sam . . . what's up?"

"Just found a piece of information I thought you might want to know."

Jake motioned to Mike to listen in.

"What's that?"

"The drone that was sent to watch the mine was definitely hacked."

"And?" said Jake.

"And . . . while the hack took place near the site, it was rerouted through a patch. That's what enabled it to actually get to the drone."

"Again," asked Jake, "and?"

"Jake . . . it was rerouted through an Arizona State Police computer."

Jake slowly turned and looked over to the corner where Garrison was talking quietly with his men, occasionally staring back at Jake and Mike.

"Thanks, Sam. Appreciate it," said Jake softly and slowly set the phone on the table. He nodded to Mike, who got up and followed him as he walked over to Garrison. "Colonel . . . I have something I want to discuss with you."

"Oh, what? You want to give me more orders, Sullivan? Is that it?"

"No . . . I just want to know how much they paid you."

"What the hell are you talking about?"

"How much did Group 45 pay you to give them access to the state computer system that controlled the drone?"

"And to keep you from hustling your ass to the site?" added Mike.

"What's the going price?" asked Jake, "to be a traitor to your country?"

"How dare you!" exclaimed Garrison.

"Come on," said Mike. "We know it was you."

Jake turned and nodded to the FBI officers, who had moved over, hands on their weapons, as they heard the argument escalate. Garrison turned to his men.

"This is all a bunch of lies! Stand your ground, men!" and the State Troopers started to form a line, with their hands on their own weapons.

Just then, one of the techs who had received a call came over to Jake with a piece of paper.

"Everyone stop!" yelled Jake.

He pointed at the State Troopers lined up behind Garrison.

"Which one of you guys is the tech guy?"

The second from the left raised his hand.

"What's his command code to enter the computer system?" said Jake, nodding at Garrison.

"You tell him nothing," said Garrison.

Jake raised his voice, "I said what's the command code!"

"C346T."

Jake looked at the piece of paper in his hand and walked over to the tech and handed it to him. The trooper looked at it and then looked at Garrison.

"That doesn't prove anything," he said.

The tech looked at Jake and nodded.

"Stand down, men," said the tech.

"You cannot disobey my order!"

"Mr. Sullivan, we'll take this from here. Colonel Garrison, you're under arrest for participating in a plot to harm the United States of America and the State of Arizona."

"You can't arrest me, you stupid son-of-a-bitch!" he said to the trooper. The trooper flung Garrison onto a table and put his hands behind his back. "I'll have your badge! You'll never be heard from again."

"You're the one that's not going to be wearing a badge anymore," and with the help of the other troopers, he moved Garrison toward the door.

"You think you're so Goddamn smart, Sullivan . . . you have no idea what you're up against. This Goddamn country is finally going to have somebody running it that knows what the hell they're doing, and I'm going to be a part of it . . . you understand?"

"Enjoy prison, Colonel. It's been a pleasure," said Jake as he turned away.

CHAPTER 43

Joe, seeing Garrison hustled out of the Yacht Club by his own men, hands cuffed behind his back, decided it was time to go. He knew he had been given a mission to take care of Sullivan and Lang, but right now they were surrounded by tactical troops, and even though he was fairly certain they didn't know about La Paz, he knew he had to get there and move things quickly, just in case.

He stuck to the shadows and made his way along the buildings and arrived at his pickup truck, certain that no one had seen him, got in, started it, and took a side road out into the desert, where he circled around Quartzsite and entered I-10 west of the town, heading to La Paz and the California border.

CHAPTER 44

It had been arranged that Mike and Jake would head directly to La Paz and hike in from the remote area where they had been directed to park their vehicle. Chestine had been kind enough to lend them her Jeep, and thanks to a full moon, they were able to drive through the desert without their lights on after leaving the main highway. Tactical was only fifteen minutes out, and there had been movement coming in from California. A dilapidated truck that appeared to be taking migrants for an early morning job had gone off I-10 and was headed to La Paz.

"Probably suicide bombers," said Mike, as he and Jake walked through the desert, dressed in black, earpieces in place so they could receive their information, and carrying automatic weapons.

As they approached the first stone ruins, they saw the dilapidated truck parked to the north next to what appeared to be a relatively new pickup. What they didn't see was a black Escalade parked farther to the north at the opposite end of the ruins where Luis had taken up position on crumbled rock that used to be a general store.

Making their way along from one pile of rock to the other, they stayed out of sight until they got into position where they could see and hear what was going on. Their suspicions had been correct.

They didn't recognize the man in the cap at first, but realized after watching him move and hearing him talk that it was Joe, who had obviously been wearing a disguise when they first met.

The migrant workers, who all appeared to be of Mid-East origin, were moving in single file with guards on each side of them to the back of the pickup where Joe was handing out a backpack to each of them. They were then being escorted to a line of vehicles that were parked on the outside of the rock outcrops for transport to their destinations. At least four armed guards were present, overseeing the operation.

Jake looked at Mike and nodded, and Mike got down close to the ground and whispered into his mouthpiece, "Confirmed. Nukes are here, being distributed. Armed guards in place. Come in hot."

CHAPTER 45

In what seemed a mere instant, two choppers appeared overhead, their lights pouring down on the scene that Jake and Mike had been observing. The guards tried to get to cover while firing at the choppers but were taken out by shooters on board.

Mike looked at Jake and said, "I'm going for our friend Joe," and made a run for the pickup truck. He arrived just at Joe was trying to open the driver's side door and jerked him backwards onto the ground. Standing over him, his automatic weapon pointed squarely in the center of Joe's forehead, he grinned.

"Okay, hero . . . here's the deal. You don't want me to pull this trigger . . . tell me . . . who's running this thing . . . and where is he?"

"It's me. There's nobody else."

"Bullshit!" said Mike. "You don't have the brains or the guts to do this!" and he fired his weapon, the rounds hitting off the rocks beside Joe's head.

"All right! All right! He's at the other end of the ruins working a computer."

"For what?"

"For the drone."

Mike spoke into his mouthpiece.

"You hear that, Jake?"

"I'm on my way!"

Meanwhile, tactical teams had come in and stopped all of the vehicles from pulling out and were rounding up the drivers and "migrant workers", taking custody of the backpacks as they did so and putting them into a specially equipped vehicle for their protection.

A sound came into Jake's and Mike's ears as they headed north.

"Sergeant Statler, Tac Team Four. We have confirmed seven satchels . . . I repeat, seven satchels . . . containing what appear to be nuclear devices, have been recovered and stored. All personnel have been accounted for. Repeat . . . all personnel accounted for."

"Almost all," said Mike, as he caught up with Jake and they moved north from one ruin to the next.

CHAPTER 46

Mike had handed off Joe to one of the tactical team members after thanking him kindly for the information he provided, before moving to catch up with Jake.

Jake put his hand on Mike to slow him down as they moved forward and pointed north where a faint blue glow illuminated from behind one of the ruins. They both came around the outcropping at the same time, one from each side, where a man dressed all in black was working at a computer.

"Put it down!" said Jake. "Now!"

"Well, well . . . Mr. Sullivan and Mr. Lang . . . I could see our good friend Joe failed to carry out his orders."

"And what might those be?" asked Mike.

"To put you two down," sneered Luis. "I knew I should have taken care of it myself."

"Speaking of being put down," said Mike, "you touch that keyboard, and you're dead!"

"Very well," Luis said, and began to raise his hands. As he did so, he picked up a rock from the loose rubble on which the computer was sitting, he backhanded the rock at Mike, who lost a second when he moved out of the way, as did Jake as he watched what happened, and Luis reached out and hit a key, as both Mike and Jake fired, driving Luis to the ground. He lay on his back, blood bubbling up out of his mouth, his teeth becoming stained with red as he smiled.

"Too late, Sullivan . . . too late . . ." and then he was gone.

Both Jake and Mike went over to the computer, which was flashing code and numbers, none of which they could understand. They picked up the laptop and handed it to one of the tactical team members who had rushed to their position.

"It's the drone. We need to figure this out and fast," said Jake. "Get Sam Walsh on this, will you?" as he handed it off to a tech.

"Will do, Mr. Sullivan."

Then they saw the phone in Luis's hand. Jake picked it up and listened. There was static . . . just a faint clicking.

"I know you're there, and I know who you are. We'll find your drone . . . and then, I promise you . . . I'll find you." With that, he threw the phone into the desert.

Trucks had pulled in to pick up those who had been captured and the bodies of those who had been killed, as had a convey, which was going to escort the truck carrying the nuclear weapons to the proving grounds at Yuma.

CHAPTER 47

Mike sat down on one of the ruins and took a deep breath.

"Looks like we did it."

"Not quite. We owe thanks to a lot of people – Chestine . . . everybody on the team. Trouble is we're missing something."

Mike nodded his head.

"I know. The drone. Where the hell is it?"

"That's what we have to find out," said Jake, "and soon. Wherever it is . . . that last nuke is with it."

Day 5

10/14

CHAPTER 48

The Leader sat in a deep leather chair on the veranda of his villa located on the ocean in the north of Cuba, an encrypted phone in his lap, and he gave thought to what had just occurred. He picked up his cane and limped over to the bar, where he poured himself a cuba libre from a pitcher sitting on the counter and walked over and sat down in front of his computer. Luis was gone. He had been a good man. He had heard it all. Sullivan and Lang . . . again they had thwarted his plans and ambitions, but he was not yet finished. He would make them pay, and in doing so, he would topple the regimes of the world's great democracies and give al-Qaeda the mushroom cloud they so desperately yearned for.

He looked at the computer and the information that Luis had sent him before his death. And the call from Sullivan . . . does he know? Perhaps . . . perhaps not. It didn't matter. They had no idea where he was. They wouldn't find him. They wouldn't stop him.

He punched in a command and off a mesa sitting outside of La Paz, Arizona, a drone came to life and received its commands, a suitcase nuke secured in its bay. He followed the track of flight that would occur tomorrow to its destination to an area just outside of Phoenix, Arizona, and the time of its arrival, at 10:25 A.M., tomorrow morning. He checked altitudes, he checked ETA for the target, and everything was in place. Then he shut it down.

Al-Qaeda would be upset. The attack would still take place on the feast day of Eid-al-Fitr, but the major California cataclysm would not occur . . . at least not yet. They would have their statement and that would be enough . . . and if it wasn't, he didn't really care. He was en route to becoming the most powerful man in the world, and they would heed his bidding, as would everyone else.

He took a sip from his cuba libre, leaned back, and smiled as he looked once again at the waves lapping at the shore. The future was on the breeze, and the future was his. It was only a matter of time.

CHAPTER 49

It was 9:30 in the morning when Jake got the call from Sam Walsh, whom he put on speaker.

"You want the good news or the bad news?"

"What is it?" asked Mike, who overheard Sam over the speaker, as did everyone who had been up the entire night working at the command post processing everything that had occurred and trying to break through the firewalls on the computer Jake and Mike had confiscated.

"The good news is I'm in. Here's the bad news. This thing is programmed to fly a low-altitude drone, which we have to assume is carrying a suitcase nuclear device. I've been able to decode its flight plan and the time of contact with its target."

"Go ahead," said Jake.

"Its flight path takes it to an area slightly outside of Phoenix, with an arrival time of 8:25 A.M., tomorrow. Its altitude at ETA is approximately one thousand feet."

"They're taking out the plane," said Jake, to no one in particular.

"What are you talking about?" asked Mike.

"Air Force One. Supposed to land at Sky Harbor at 8:30 A.M."

"I've calculated the altitudes, Jake. It's going to hit it as it's landing."

"That's all good stuff. We can redirect the drone, then," said Mike. "You're in."

"That's more bad news. I don't have control. There's another firewall, and I haven't been able to hack it."

"Wait," said Mike, "this is set for tomorrow . . . that drone can't be in the air yet. We have time to find it."

"Sorry, Mike," said Sam. "Group 45 has done a good job on this. I can't get any kind of signal out of it. Whoever programmed this thing put in an automatic shutdown and an automatic restart. This thing could be anywhere in the Arizona desert just sitting there until tomorrow morning, when it will take off and head for its destination."

Mike looked at Jake and yelled into the speaker, "Sam, we can't just sit here and do nothing!"

"If I were you," said Sam, "I would concentrate my search around La Paz. Other than that, the only thing we can do is notify the President."

"Do your best, Sam," said Jake. "Try to get in. I'm calling Jason Bates."

"Will do, Mr. Sullivan. I'll get back to you as soon as I have anything."

Mike slammed his hand on the table.

"I can't believe we can't do anything!"

"Do what he said," said Jake. "Send the tactical teams out around La Paz and have them move out in every direction. Maybe we'll get lucky . . . but it's a long-shot at best." Then he turned to one of the tech people and said, "Get me Jason Bates on the line."

CHAPTER 50

"Christ, Sullivan! How could this happen?" said Bates. "A nuclear attack on Air Force One? Seems impossible."

"I know, Jason. At least we stopped the attack on California."

"Yeah, I know . . . I know. Walsh gave me the whole scenario. If that thing goes off over Phoenix . . ."

"And the President?" asked Jake.

"You know him . . . if this was just himself he had to worry about, we'd be lifting off tomorrow morning, but given that we have the fate of all the leaders of the free world in our hands, he's agreed to hold the G8 here in Washington. We've created an excuse that two of the leaders have developed the flu and can't fly. It gives us a little bit of cover, anyway."

"Sounds believable," said Jake.

"Best we can do on such short notice."

"Jason, if we don't find this thing and it gets airborne, we will have to try and shoot it down."

"I know . . . I know. The President has given the order. Jets will scramble on his command. As soon as you have any indication that thing is in the air, we'll know . . . we're all hooked into the same computer. We can see the clock running. Look, I really hope we can talk about this at 8:26 A.M., tomorrow morning, all right? In the meantime, do that thing you do, will you. Find this thing before it gets airborne."

"That's a big desert out there, Jason."

"I know, and I don't want Phoenix to become a part of it."

The line went dead. They both knew there was nothing else to say.

Day 0

10/15

CHAPTER 51

The previous day's hunt through the desert had proven futile. Ground searches had come up empty and fly-overs had not been able to obtain a heat signature or a sighting.

Group 45 had been diligent in their preparation, as usual.

Search planes had flown directly over the mesa where the drone was sitting, but it was sitting under a camouflage tent that had been matched exactly to the top of the surface of the mesa that completely shielded the drone and it could not be discerned with an overhead flight.

The command center at the Yacht Club had been patched in so that all parties were on speaker with each other at all times as they prepared for the worst.

President Fletcher and Bates were in the Oval Office. The fighter wing at Luke Air Force Base in Glendale was patched in and Sam Walsh, who had been up all night, was still trying to hack into the drone.

At exactly 8:20 A.M., his excited voice came online.

"I'm in! I'm in!"

"You have control?" asked Jake.

"Not yet, but I'm through the firewall. This thing came to life and to ready itself for ignition, all its firewalls came down. Speaking of which, it just lifted off."

And it was true. The tarp that had concealed the drone blew away with the force of ignition as the drone lifted off the mesa into the air.

Lieutenant Colonel James Collodi, who was in command of three F-15 fighter jets ordered take off from Luke Air Force Base and locked on to the computer screen, following the path of the drone.

At 8:21 a voice came into his earpiece.

"Lieutenant Colonel Collodi . . . this is President Fletcher."

"Yes, sir," said Collodi.

"You going to take care of this for me, Lieutenant Colonel?"

"Yes, sir," replied Collodi.

"Our prayers are with you. Now, go get me that drone."

"Roger that, sir," and communications ended.

Collodi led his group on the flight path as set out in the computer program as the clock ticked to 8:22. By then they had arrived at the point where the drone should be, but it was nowhere in sight. Collodi reported in to command headquarters.

"No drone in sight. Repeat . . . no drone in sight."

"What the hell is going on?" asked Mike.

"Diversion . . . it's another diversion!" yelled Sam Walsh.

Jake looked at the clock. It was 8:22:15.

"Jake! The computer is fake. It's not controlling the drone. There is another program that was entered yesterday. The program is imbedded and final . . . whomever did it can't shut it down."

"Hurry up, Sam. What are you doing?"

"Eliminating air craft. I've got it! Colonel! I'm going to give you coordinates. Get there as fast as you can. It's only about a half mile away."

"Will do."

Another desperate twenty seconds were lost, and then Collodi's voice came back on.

"We have visual contact. The drone is taking evasive action. Do I have the order to engage? Repeat . . . do I have the order to engage?"

The voice of Jason Bates came online.

"The President has given his order. Colonel . . . engage. I repeat . . . engage."

"Wait! Wait!" yelled a frantic Sam Walsh. "Do not engage! Do not engage!"

"What the hell is going on out there, Jake?" said Bates. "The President gave his order."

"Sam?!" yelled Jake.

"I'm in! The nukes been wired into the system. It's controlled by a sensor. Any contact with that drone's field will detonate the nuke. If a jet tries to take it out, it will explode, and it's flying at the altitude where it will do the utmost damage."

"Sam," said Mike, "are you telling us that if this thing even falls to the ground, that nuke's going to go off?"

"Exactly," said Sam.

"So we're out of options?" asked Mike.

"Not yet," said Sam. "I'm trying . . . I'm almost there."

The clock now read 8:24.

"I got it! I have control of the flight mechanisms!" yelled Sam Walsh over the loudspeaker, and a roar went up from the room. "Jake," yelled Sam above the applause that began, "listen, we have a problem."

Jake hushed the room.

"What is it, Sam?"

"I'm trying, but I don't have it disarmed yet."

There was silence. Jake looked around.

"Jake, we don't have time to get it to the Pacific. The max speed for this thing is three hundred miles per hour. I checked the coordinates. The straightest path . . . is still three hundred and seven miles away. There's no time."

"Colonel, you might want to get your men out. I'm going to take this thing to the most isolated spot in the desert I can find."

Again there was silence, and then Colonel Collodi's voice came on.

"We'll ride it out. You may need us."

"Colonel, you know what this means . . ."

"You heard me, son."

The clock now read 8:24:30.

Mike looked at Jake and spoke in a soft voice.

"No time. Can't evacuate. Can't do anything."

And they watched the seconds tick down to 8:24:45. There was silence.

In Washington, Bates looked at President Fletcher, and they both hung their heads, knowing there was nothing they could do.

The same was happening in Phoenix and in Quartzsite, Arizona.

"You know we're . . ." Mike started to say.

"I know," said Jake, "I know. We're in the blast zone."

"I don't know what to . . ." Mike started to say, when a voice came over the speaker.

"Colonel, I want you to be my eyes. I'm going to set this drone on the ground. I'm pretty sure I've disarmed it."

"Pretty sure?" asked Mike, looking at Jake.

Jake just shrugged.

"You've got nothing but open desert below you, Mr. Walsh. Do your best."

"Here we go," said Sam, and just then, the clock read 8:25.

"Mr. Walsh," came the voice of Lieutenant Colonel Collodi, "the drone is safely landed in the Arizona desert, and there has been no explosion, as I am sure you are aware."

It was funny, but this time there was no cheer. There was no applause. There was just a sigh of relief from everyone who had been involved, and then the voice of President Fletcher came on the line.

"Mr. Walsh, your country owes you a great deal. I will see you in Washington."

"Thank you, Mr. President."

"Jake and Mike, as always . . ."

"Yes, sir," replied Jake and Mike in unison.

"Colonel Collodi . . ."

"Mr. President?"

"I want that nuke."

"Already sent orders to Yuma, sir. Tactical team is on the way. We're circling it until it arrives. Nobody's getting to that drone before we do."

"Thank you, Lieutenant Colonel . . . and thank your brave men for me."

"It's been a pleasure, Mr. President," and then there was radio silence.

And in a chair on the veranda on the north shore of Cuba, a man slumped back, a computer key pad dropped to his feet, and bile ran in this throat as the enormity of his defeat overcame him.

CHAPTER 52

There was a celebration that night at the Quartzsite Yacht Club, closed to the general public, but a group of men and women had averted disaster and the tension gave way to laughter, emotion, and food and drink supplied by the kind and considerate MeMe Selleck, who had been sworn to secrecy about the entire matter.

Jake and Mike had each given her their utmost thanks and were rewarded with memberships in the Quartzsite Yacht Club.

"I've got to tell you, MeMe," said Jake, "this is undoubtedly one of the best things I've ever been a member of."

"Thank you. I appreciate it."

She handed one to Mike, who gave her a kiss on the cheek.

"Thanks, MeMe, for everything."

"You boys are welcome back here any time, so don't be strangers."

"We promise," said Jake, "we'll be back."

They both hugged Chestine and thanked her for all she had done.

"You saved the day," said Mike.

"Lucky guess," she said. "Just happy it worked out."

"You are one smart young lady," said Jake. "It wasn't a guess. You saved everybody. We couldn't have done it without you."

"Glad I could help. You guys don't do too bad yourselves," and they laughed and hugged, and the party went on. But after a while, Jake wandered outside and stood in the cool night air, the desert stretching in front of him, illuminated a ghostly white by the full moon overhead. Mike came out.

"What is it, Jake? What's bothering you?"

"Nothing. Just tired, I think."

"I know you too well. What's going on?"

"He stepped up his game, Mike. He was ready to take out the leaders of the free world, kill millions of people, and destroy this country. He wants it all."

"What are you talking about?"

"Antonio Ortiz. They never found his body, Mike. It's him. I know it. He's going to keep trying. We have to stop him."

"We will, Jake. We always do."

"It was close this time, Mike. Too close."

Mike walked up and put his hand on Jake's shoulder."

"Do yourself a favor, my friend. Take one night off, okay? Enjoy these people. Enjoy what we did. And we'll wake up tomorrow and we'll start over again . . . and we'll get him."

Jake looked at him and smiled.

"All right?"

"Yeah, all right. You got it. C'mon . . . let's go back inside."

And they did. And the party went on.

CHAPTER 53

The Leader stood on the veranda, leaning against the railing, his cuba libre nearly done. He had been standing too long and the pain in his leg was increasing. His temples were throbbing as he went over and over everything . . . the total failure he had endured. He yelled out in pain and frustration and hurled the glass toward the ocean, hobbled back, and fell into his chair. He closed his eyes, the anger growing, and he made a vow.

"This will not happen again. It is time to put an end to Jake Sullivan and Mike Lang. The day of reckoning is coming."

And he looked up at the same moon that shown on the Arizona desert and for the briefest of moments, he felt the presence of his enemy, and he said again, "It's coming."

EPILOGUE

CHAPTER 54

Newsflash: February 3, 2018. The *Daily Mail* reports that Konstantin Sivkov, a Russian military analyst, has said that his country should develop weapons that can cause tsunamis and volcanic eruptions in the United States. The Russian analyst reasoned because eighty percent of the United States population lives near the coast, generating a tsunami on the San Andreas Fault would be an effective way of causing damage to millions of people. Detonating nuclear weapons on the fault would unleash tsunamis that would have a devastating effect.

COMING FALL 2018

CHIP BELL

1725 FIFTH AVENUE
ARNOLD, PA 15068

724-339-2355

chip.bell.author@gmail.com
clb.bcymlaw@verizon.net
www.ChipBellAuthor.com

 FOLLOW ME ON FACEBOOK
facebook.com/chipbellauthor

 FOLLOW ME ON TWITTER
@ChipBellAuthor

 FOLLOW ME ON PINTEREST
pinterest.com/chipbellauthor
/the-jake-sullivan-series

Made in the USA
Monee, IL
16 May 2025